Resounding Praise for *Fine Just the Way It Is*

Fine Just the Way It Is

WYOMING STORIES 3

ANNIE PROULX

SCRIBNER
New York   London   Toronto   Sydney

SCRIBNER
A Division of Simon & Schuster, Inc.
1230 Avenue of the Americas
New York, NY 10020

First Scribner trade paperback edition September 2009

SCRIBNER and design are registered trademarks of The Gale Group, Inc. used under license by Simon & Schuster, Inc., the publisher of this work.

For information about special discounts for bulk purchases, please contact Simon & Schuster Special Sales at 1-866-506-1949 or business@simonandschuster.com.

The Simon & Schuster Speakers Bureau can bring authors to your live event. For more information or to book an event contact the Simon & Schuster Speakers Bureau at 1-866-248-3049 or visit our website at www.simonspeakers.com.

DESIGNED BY ERICH HOBBING

Manufactured in the United States of America

3 5 7 9 10 8 6 4

Library of Congress Cataloging-in-Publication Data

ISBN: 978-1-4165-7166-7
ISBN: 978-1-4165-7167-4 (pbk)

A version of "Family Man" was first published in *Granta*.

For Muffy & Geoff

Jon & Gail

Gillis

Morgan

Contents

On the surface, everything was lovely, but when you got into the inside circle you soon found out that the lines of demarcation were plainly marked.

—John Clay, *My Life on the Range*

Fine Just
the Way It Is

Family Man

The Mellowhorn Home was a rambling one-story log building identifying itself as western—the furniture upholstered
in fabrics with geometric "Indian" designs, lampshades sporting
buckskin fringe. On the walls hung Mr. Mellowhorn's mounted
mule deer heads and a two-man crosscut saw.

It was the time of year when Berenice Pann became conscious
of the earth's dark turning, not a good time, she thought, to be
starting a job, especially one as depressing as caring for elderly
ranch widows. But she took what she could get. There were not
many men in the Mellowhorn Retirement Home, and those
few were so set upon by the women that Berenice pitied them.
She had believed the sex drive faded in the elderly, but these
crones vied for the favors of palsied men with beef jerky arms.
The men could take their pick of shapeless housecoats and flowery skeletons.

Three deceased and stuffed Mellowhorn dogs stood in strate-
gic guard positions—near the front door, at the foot of the stairs,
and beside the rustic bar made from old fence posts. Small signs,
the product of the pyrographer's art, preserved their names:
Joker, Bugs and Henry. At least, thought Berenice, patting Henry's
head, the Home had a view of the enclosing mountains. It had
rained all day and now, in the stiffening gloom, tufts of bunchgrass

showed up like bleached hair. Down along an old irrigation ditch willows made a ragged line of somber maroon, and the stock pond at the bottom of the hill was as flat as zinc. She went to another window to look at coming weather. In the northwest a wedge of sky, milk-white and chill, herded the rain before it. An old man sat at the community room window staring out at the grey autumn. Berenice knew his name, knew all their names; Ray Forkenbrock.

"Get you something, Mr. Forkenbrock?" She made a point of prefacing the names of residents with the appropriate honorifics, something the rest of the staff did not do, slinging around first names as though they'd all grown up together. Deb Slaver was familiar to a fault, chumming up with "Sammy," and "Rita" and "Delia," punctuated with "Hon," "Sweetie" and "Babes."

"Yeah," he said. He spoke with long pauses between sentences, a slow unfurling of words that made Berenice want to jump in with word suggestions.

"Get me the hell out a here," he said.

"Get me a horse," he said.

"Get me seventy year back a ways," said Mr. Forkenbrock.

"I can't do that, but I can get you a nice cup of tea. And it'll be Social Hour in ten minutes," she said.

She couldn't quite meet his stare. He was something to look at, despite an ordinary face with infolded lips, a scrawny neck. It was the eyes. They were very large and wide open and of the palest, palest blue, the color of ice chipped with a pick, faint blue with crystalline rays. In photographs they appeared white like the eyes of Roman statues, saved from that blind stare only by the black dots of pupils. When he looked at you, thought Berenice, you could not understand a word he said for being fixed by those strange white eyes. She did not like him but pretended she did. Women had to pretend to like men and to admire the things they liked. Her own sister had married a man who was interested in rocks and now she had to drag around deserts and steep mountains with him.

At Social Hour the residents could have drinks and crackers smeared with cheese paste from the Super Wal-Mart where Cook shopped. They were all lushes, homing in on the whiskey bottle. Chauncey Mellowhorn, who had built the Mellowhorn Retirement Home and set all policy, believed that the last feeble years should be enjoyed, and promoted smoking, drinking, lascivious television programs and plenty of cheap food. Neither teetotalers nor bible thumpers signed up for the Mellowhorn Retirement Home.

Ray Forkenbrock said nothing. Berenice thought he looked sad and she wanted to cheer him up in some way.

"What did you used to do, Mr. Forkenbrock? Were you a rancher?"

The old man glared up at her. "No," he said. "I wasn't no goddamn rancher. I was a hand," he said.

"I worked for them sonsabitches. Cowboyed, ran wild horses, rodeoed, worked in the oil patch, sheared sheep, drove trucks, did whatever," he said. "Ended up broke."

"Now my granddaughter's husband pays the bills that keep me here in this nest of old women," he said. He often wished he had died out in the weather, alone and no trouble to anyone.

Berenice continued, making her voice cheery. "I had a lot a different jobs too since I graduated high school," she said. "Waitress, day care, housecleaning, Seven-Eleven store clerk, like that." She was engaged to Chad Grills; they were to be married in the spring and she planned to keep working only for a little while to supplement Chad's paycheck from Red Bank Power. But before the old man could say anything more Deb Slaver came pushing in, carrying a glass. Berenice could smell the dark whiskey. Deb's vigorous voice pumped out of her ample chest in jets.

"Here you go, honey-boy! A nice little drinkie for Ray!" she said. "Turn around from that dark old winder and have some fun!" She said, "Don't you want a watch *Cops* with Powder Face?" (Powder Face was Deb's nickname for a painted harridan with hazelnut knuckles and a set of tawny teeth.) "Or is it just one a them days when you want a look out the winder and feel blue? Think of some troubles? You retired folks don't know what trouble is, just setting here having a nice glass of whiskey and watching teevee," she said.

She punched the pillows on the settee. "We're the ones with troubles—bills, cheating husbands, sassy kids, tired feet," she said. "Trying to scrape up the money for winter tires! My husband says the witch with the green teeth is plaguing us," she said. "Come on, I'll set with you and Powder Face awhile," and she pulled Mr. Forkenbrock by his sweater, threw him onto the settee and sat beside him.

Berenice left the room and went to help in the kitchen, where the cook was smacking out turkey patties. A radio on the windowsill murmured.

"Looks like it is clearing up," Berenice said. She was a little afraid of the cook.

"Oh good, you're here. Get them French fry packages out of the freezer," she said. "Thought I was going to have to do everthing myself. Deb was supposed to help, but she rather tangle up with them old boys. She hopes they'll put her in their will. Some of them's got a little property or a mineral-rights check coming in," she said. "You ever meet her husband, Duck Slaver?" Now she was grating a cabbage into a stainless steel bowl.

Berenice knew only that Duck Slaver drove a tow truck for

Ricochet Towing. The radio suddenly caught the cook's attention and she turned up the volume, hearing that it would be cloudy the next day with gradual clearing, the following day high winds and snow showers.

"We ought to be grateful for the rain in this drought. Know what Bench says?" Bench was the UPS driver, the source of Cook's information on everything from road conditions to family squabbles.

"No."

"Says we are in the beginning of turning into a desert. It's all going to blow away," she said.

When Berenice went to announce dinner—turkey patties, French fries (Mr. Mellowhorn still called them "freedom fries") with turkey patty gravy, cranberry relish, creamed corn and homemade rolls—she saw that Deb had worked Mr. Forkenbrock into the corner of the settee, and Powder Face was in the chair with the bad leg watching cops squash the faces of black men onto sidewalks. Mr. Forkenbrock was staring at the dark window, the coursing raindrops catching the blue television flicker. He gave off an aura of separateness. Deb and Powder Face might have been two more of Mellowhorn's stuffed dogs.

After dinner, on her way back to the kitchen to help the cook clean up, Berenice opened the door for a breath of fresh air. The eastern half of the sky was starry, the west a slab of basalt.

In the early morning darkness the rain began again. He did not know but would have understood the poet's line "I wake and feel the fell of dark, not day." Nothing in nature seemed more malign to Ray Forkenbrock than this invisible crawl of weather, the blunt-nosed cloud advancing under the lid of darkness. As the dim morning emerged, like a photograph in developing solution, the sound of the rain sharpened. That's sleet, he thought, remembering a long October ride in such weather when he was young, his denim jacket soaked through and sparkling with ice, remembered meeting up with that old horse catcher who lived out in the desert, must have been in his eighties, out there in the rattling precip limping along, heading for the nearest ranch bunkhouse, he said, to get out of the weather.

"That'd be Flying A," said Ray, squinting against the slanting ice.

"Ain't that Hawkins's place?"

"Naw. Hawkins sold out couple years ago. A fella named Fox owns it now," he said.

"Hell, I lose touch out here. Had a pretty good shack up until day before yesterday," the horse catcher said between clicking teeth and went on to tell that his place had burned down and he'd slept out in the sage for two nights but now his bedroll was soaked and he was out of food. Ray felt bad for him and at the same time wanted to get away. It seemed awkward to be mounted while the man was afoot, but then he always had that same uncomfortable, guilty itch when he rode past a pedestrian. Was it his fault the old man didn't have a horse? If he was any good at horse catching he should have had a hundred of them. He foraged through his pockets and found three or four stale peanuts mixed with lint.

"It ain't much but it's all I got," he said, holding them out.

The old boy had never made it to the Flying A. He was discovered days later sitting with his back against a rock. Roy remembered the uncomfortable feeling he'd had exchanging a few words with him, thinking how old he was. Now he was the same age, and he had reached the Flying A—the warmth and dry shelter of the Mellowhorn Home. But the old horse catcher's death, braced against a rock, seemed more honorable.

It was six-thirty and there was nothing to get up for, but he put on his jeans and shirt, added an old man's sweater as the dining room could be chilly in the morning before the heat got going, left his boots in the closet and shuffled down the hall in red felt slippers, too soft to deliver a kick to stuffed Bugs with the googly eyes at the foot of the stairs. The slippers were a gift from his only granddaughter, Beth, married to Kevin Bead. Beth was important to him. He had made up his mind to tell her the ugly family secret. He would not leave his descendants to grapple with shameful uncertainties. He was going to clear the air. Beth was coming on Saturday afternoon with her tape recorder to help him get it said. During the week she would type it into her computer and bring him the crisp printed pages. He might have been nothing more than a ranch hand in his life, but he knew a few things.

Beth was dark-haired with very red cheeks that looked freshly slapped. It was the Irish in her he supposed. She bit her fingernails, an unsightly habit in a grown woman. Her husband, Kevin, worked in the loan department of the High Plains Bank. He complained that his job was stupid, tossing money and credit cards to people who could never pay up.

"Used to be to get a card you had to work hard and have good credit. Now the worse your credit the easier it is to get a dozen of them," he said to his wife's grandfather. Ray, who had never had a credit card, couldn't follow the barrage of expository information that followed about changing bank rules, debt. These information sessions always ended with Kevin sighing and saying in a dark tone that the day was coming.

Ray Forkenbrock guessed Beth would use the computer at the real estate office where she worked to transcribe his words.

"Oh no, Grandpa, we've got a computer and printer at home.

Rosalyn wouldn't like for me to do it in the office," she said. Rosalyn was her boss, a woman Ray had never seen but felt he knew well because Beth talked often about her. She was very, very fat and had financial trouble. Scam artists several times stole her identity. Every few months she spent hours filling out fraud affidavits. And, said Beth, she wore XXXL blue jeans and a belt with a silver buckle as big as a pie tin that she had won at a bingo game.

Ray snorted. "A buckle used to mean something," he said. "A rodeo buckle, best part of the prize. The money was nothing in them days," he said. "We didn't care about the money. We cared about the buckle," he said, "and now fat gals win them at bingo games?" He twisted his head around and looked at the closet door. Beth knew he must have a belt with a rodeo buckle in there.

"Do you watch the National Finals on television?" she said. "Or the bull-riding championship?"

"Hell, no," he said. "The old hens here wouldn't put up with it. They got that teevee lined out from dawn to midnight—crime, that reality shit, fashion and python shows, dog and cat programs. Watch rodeo? Not a chance," he said.

He glared at the empty hall beyond the open door. "You wouldn't never guess the most of them lived on ranches all their life," he added sourly.

Beth spoke to Mr. Mellowhorn and said she thought her grandfather could at least watch the National Finals or the PBR rodeos considering what they were paying for his keep. Mr. Mellowhorn agreed.

"But I like to keep out of residents' television choices, you know, democracy rules at the Mellowhorn Home, and if your grandfather wants to watch rodeo all he has to do is persuade a majority of the inhabitants to sign a petition and—"

"Do you have any objection if my husband and I get him a television set for his room?"

"Well, no, of course not, but I should just mention that the less fortunate residents might see him as privileged, even a little high-hat if he holes up in his room and watches rodeo instead of joining the community choice—"

"Fine," said Beth, cutting past the social tyranny of the Mellowhorn Home. "That's what we'll do, then. Get him a snooty, high-hat television. Family counts with me and Kevin," she said. "I don't suppose you have a satellite hookup, do you?" she asked.

"Well, no. We've discussed it, but—maybe next year—"

She brought Ray a small television set with a DVD player and three or four discs of recent years' rodeo events. That got him going.

"Christ, I remember when the finals was in Oklahoma City, not goddamn Las Vegas," he said. "Of course bull riding has pushed out all the other events now, good-bye saddle bronc and bareback. I was there when Freckles Brown rode Tornado in 1962," he said. "Forty-six year old, and the ones they got now bull riding are children! Make a million dollars. It's all show business now," he said. "The old boys was a rough crew. Heavy drinkers, most of them. You want to know what pain is, try bull riding with a bad hangover."

"So I guess you did a lot of rodeo riding when you were young?"

"No, not a lot, but enough to get broke up some. And earned a buckle," he said. "You heal fast when you're young, but the broke places sort of come back to life when you are old. I busted my left leg in three places. Hurts now when it rains," he said.

"How come you cowboyed for a living, Grandpa Ray? Your daddy wasn't a rancher or a cowboy, was he?" She turned the volume knob down. The riders came out of a chute, again and again, monotonously, all apparently wearing the same dirty hat.

"Hell no, he wasn't. He was a coal miner. Rove Forkenbrock," he said. "My mother's name was Alice Grand Forkenbrock. Dad worked in the Union Pacific coal mines. Something happened to him and he quit. Moved into running errands for different outfits, Texaco, California Petroleum, big outfits.

"Anyway, don't exactly know what the old man did. Drove a dusty old Model T. He'd get fired and then he had to scratch around for another job. Even though he drank—that's what got him fired usually—he always seemed to get another job pretty quick." He swallowed a little whiskey.

"Anymore I wouldn't go near the mines. I liked horses almost as much as I liked arithmetic, liked the cow business, so after I graduated eighth grade and Dad said better forget high school, things were tough and I had to find work," he said. "At the time I didn't mind. What my dad said I generally didn't fuss over. I respected him. I respected and honored my father. I believed him to be a good and fair man." He thought, unaccountably, of weeds.

"I tried for a job and got took on at Bledsoe's Double B," he said. "The bunkhouse life. The Bledsoes more or less raised me to voting age. At that point I sure didn't want nothing to do with my family," he said and fell into an old man's reverie. Weeds, weeds and wildness.

Beth was quiet for a few minutes, then chatted about her boys. Syl had acted the part of an eagle in a school play and what a job, making the costume! Just before she left she said offhandedly, "You know, I want my boys to know about their great-granddad. What do you think if I bring my recorder and get it on tape and then type it up? It would be like a book of your life—something for the future generations of the family to read and know about."

He laughed in derision.

"Some of it ain't so nice to know. Every family got its dirty laundry and we got ours." But after a week of thinking about it, of wondering why he'd kept it bottled up for so long, he told Beth to bring on her machine.

They sat in his little room with the door closed.

"'Antisocial,' they'll say. Everybody else sits with the door open hollering at each other's folks as if they was all related somehow. A regional family, they call it here. I like my privacy."

She put a glass of whiskey, another of water and the tape recorder, smaller than a pack of cigarettes, on the table near his elbow and said, "It's on, Grandpa. Tell me how it was growing up in the old days. Just talk any time you are ready."

He cleared his throat and began slowly, watching the spiky volume meter jump. "I'm eighty-four years old and most of them involved in the early days has gone on before, so it don't make much difference what I tell." He took a nervous swallow of the whiskey and nodded.

"I was fourteen year old in nineteen and thirty-three and there wasn't a nickel in the world." The silence of that time before traffic and leaf blowers and the boisterous shouting of television was embedded in his character, and he spoke little, finding it hard to drag out the story. The noiselessness of his youth except for the natural sound of wind, hoofbeats, the snap of the old house logs splitting in winter cold, wild herons crying their way downriver was forever lost. How silent men and women had been in those times, trusting to observational powers. There had been days when a few little mustache clouds moved, and he could imagine them making no more sound than dragging a feather across a wire. The wind got them and the sky was alone.

"When I was a kid we lived hard, let me tell you. Coalie Town, about eight miles from Superior. It's all gone now," he said.

"Three-room shack, no insulation, kids always sick. My baby sister Goldie died of meningitis in that shack," he said.

Now he was warming up to his sorry tale. "No water. A truck used to come every week and fill up a couple barrels we had. Mama paid a quarter a barrel. No indoor plumbing. People make jokes about it now but it was miserable to go out there to that outhouse on a bitter morning with the wind screaming up the hole. Christ," he said. He was silent for so long Beth backed up the tape and pressed the pause button on the recorder. He lit a cigarette, sighed, abruptly started talking again. Beth lost a sentence or two before she got the recorder restarted.

"People thought they was doing all right if they was alive. You can learn to eat dust instead of bread, my mother said many a time. She had a lot a old sayings. Is that thing on?" he said.

"Yes, Grandpa," she said. "It is on. Just talk."

"Bacon," he said. "She'd say if bacon curls in the pan the hog was butchered wrong side of the moon. We didn't see bacon very often and it could of done corkscrews in the pan, would have been okay with us long as we could eat it," he said.

"There was a whole bunch a shacks out there near the mines. They called it Coalie Town. Lot of foreigners."

"As I come up," he said, "I got a pretty good education in fighting, screwing—pardon my French—and more fighting. Every problem was solved with a fight. I remember all them people. Pattersons, Bob Hokker, the Grainblewer twins, Alex Sugar, Forrie Wintka, Harry and Joe Dolan . . . We had a lot of fun. Kids always have fun," he said.

"They sure do," said Beth.

"Kids don't get all sour thinking about the indoor toilets they don't have, or moaning because there ain't no fresh butter. For us everthing was fine the way it was. I had a happy childhood. When we got bigger there was certain girls. Forrie Wintka. Really good looking, long black hair and black eyes," he said, looking to see if he had shocked her.

"She finally married old man Dolan after his wife died. The Dolan boys was something else. They hated each other, fought, really had bad fights, slugged each other with boards with nails in the end, heaved rocks."

Beth tried to shift him to a description of his own family, but he went on about the Dolans.

"I'm pretty set in my ways," he said. She nodded.

"One time Joe knocked Harry out, kicked him into the Platte. He could of drowned, probably would of but Dave Arthur was riding along the river, seen this bundle of rags snarled up in a cottonwood sweeper—it had fell in the river and caught up all sorts of river trash. He thought maybe some clothes. Went to see and pulled Harry out," he said.

"Harry was about three-quarters dead, never was right after that, neither. But right enough to know that his own brother had meant to kill him. Joe couldn't never tell if Harry was going to be around the next corner with a chunk of wood or a gun." There was a long pause after the word "gun."

"Nervous wreck," he said. He watched the tape revolve for long seconds.

"Dutchy Green was my best friend in grade school. He was killed when he was twenty-five, twenty-six, shooting at some of them old Indian rock carvings. The ricochet got him through the right temple," he said.

He took a swallow of whiskey. "Yep, our family. There was my mother. She was tempery, too much to do and no money to do it. Me, the oldest. There was a big brother, Sonny, but he drowned in an irrigation ditch before I come along," he said.

"Weren't there girls in the family?" asked Beth. Not content with two sons, she craved a daughter.

"My sisters, Irene and Daisy. Irene lives in Greybull and Daisy is still alive out in California. And I mentioned, the baby Goldie died when I was around six or seven. The youngest survivor was Roger. Mama's last baby. He went the wrong way. Did time for robbing," he said. "No idea what happened to him." Under the weeds, damned and dark.

Abruptly he veered away from the burglar brother. "You got to understand that I loved my dad. We all did. Him and Mother was always kissing and hugging and laughing when he was home. He was a wonderful man with kids, always a big smile and a hug, remembered all your interests, lots of times brought home special little presents. I still got every one he give me." His voice trembled like that of the old horse catcher in the antique sleet.

"Remembering this stuff makes me tired. I guess I better stop," he said. "Anymore two new people come in today and the new ones always makes me damn tired."

"Women or men?" asked Beth, relieved to turn the recorder off as she could see her only tape was on short time. She remembered now she had recorded the junior choir practice.

"Don't know," he said. "Find out at supper."

"I'll come next week. I think what you are saying is important for this family." She kissed his dry old man's forehead, brown age spots.

"Just wait," he said.

After she left he started talking again as if the tape were still running. "He died age forty-seven. I thought that was real old. Why didn't he jump?" he said.

Berenice Pann, bearing a still-warm chocolate cupcake, paused outside his door when she heard his voice. She had seen Beth leave a few minutes earlier. Maybe she had forgotten something and come back. Berenice heard something like a strangled sob from Mr. Forkenbrock. "God, it was lousy," he said. "So we could work. Hell, I liked school. No chance when you start work at thirteen," he said. "Wasn't for the Bledsoes I'd ended up a bum," he said to himself. "Or worse."

Berenice Pann's boyfriend, Chad Grills, was the great-grandson of the old Bledsoes. They were still on the ranch where Ray Forkenbrock had worked in his early days, both of them over the century mark. Berenice became an avid eavesdropper, feeling that in a way she was related to Mr. Forkenbrock through the Bledsoes. She owed it to herself and Chad to hear as much as she could about the Bledsoes, good or bad. Inside the room there was silence, then the door flung open.

"Uh!" cried Berenice, the cupcake sliding on its saucer. "I was just bringing you this—"

"That so?" said Mr. Forkenbrock. He took the cupcake from the saucer and instead of taking a sample bite crammed the whole thing into his mouth, paper cup and all. The paper massed behind his dentures.

At the Social Hour, Mr. Mellowhorn arrived to introduce the new "guests." Church Bollinger was a younger man, barely sixty-five, but Roy could tell he was a real slacker. He'd obviously come into the Home because he couldn't get up the gumption to make his own bed or wash his dishes. The other one, Mrs. Terry Taylor, was around his age, early eighties despite the dyed red hair and carmine fingernails. She seemed soft and sagging, somehow like a candle standing in the sun. She kept looking at Ray. Her eyes were khaki-colored, the lashes sparse and short, her thin old lips greased up with enough lipstick to leave red on her buttered roll. Finally he could take her staring no longer.

"Got a question?" he said.

"Are you Ray Forkenknife?" she said.

"Forkenbrock," he said, startled.

"Oh, right. Forkenbrock. You don't remember me? Theresa Worley? From Coalie Town? Me and you went to school together except you was a couple grades ahead."

But he did not remember her.

The next morning, fork poised over the poached egg reclining like a houri on a bed of soggy toast, he glanced up to meet her intense gaze. Her red-slick lips parted to show ocher teeth that were certainly her own, for no dentist would make dentures that looked as though they had been dredged from a sewage pit.

"Don't you remember Mrs. Wilson?" she said. "The teacher that got froze in a blizzard looking for her cat? The Skeltcher kids that got killed when they fell in a old mine shaft?"

He did remember something about a schoolteacher frozen in a June blizzard but thought it had happened somewhere else, down around Cold Mountain. As for the Skeltcher kids, he denied them and shook his head.

On Saturday Beth came again, and again set out the glass of water, the glass of whiskey and the tape recorder. He had been thinking what he wanted to say. It was clear enough in his head, but putting it into words was difficult. The whole thing had been so subtle and painful it was impossible to present it without sounding like a fool. And Mrs. Terry Taylor, a.k.a. Theresa Worley, had sidelined him. He strove to remember the frozen teacher, the Skeltcher kids in the mine shaft, how Mr. Baker had shot Mr. Dennison over a bushel of potatoes and a dozen other tragedies

she had laid out as mnemonic bait. He remembered very different events. He remembered walking to the top of Irish Hill with
Dutchy Green to meet Forrie Wintka, who was going to show
them her private parts in exchange for a nickel each. It was late
autumn, the cottonwoods leafless along the grim trickle of Coal
Creek, warm weather holding. They could see Forrie Wintka
toiling up from the shacks below. Dutchy said it would be easy,
not only would she show them, they could do it to her, even her
brother did it to her.

Dutchy whispered as though she could hear them. "Even her
stepfather. He got killed by a mountain line last year."

And now, seventy-one years later, it hit him. Her father had
been Worley, Wintka was the stepfather who had carried the mail
horseback and in Snakeroot Canyon had been dragged into the
rocks by a lion. The first female he had ever plowed, a coal
town slut, was sharing final days with him at the Mellowhorn
Home.

"Beth," he said to his granddaughter. "I can't talk about nothing today. There's some stuff come to mind just now that I got to
think my way through. The new woman who come here last
week. I knew her and it wasn't under the best circumstances," he
said. That was the trouble with Wyoming; everything you ever
did or said kept pace with you right to the end. The regional family again.

Mr. Mellowhorn started a series of overnight outings he dubbed
"Weekend Adventures." The first one had been to the Medicine
Wheel up in the Big Horns. Mrs. Wallace Kimes had fallen and
scraped her knees on the crushed stone in the parking lot. Then
came the dude ranch weekend where the Mellowhorn group
found itself sharing the premises with seven elk hunters from

Colorado, most of them drunk and disorderly and given over to senseless laughter topping 110 decibels. Powder Face laughed senselessly with them. The third trip was more ambitious; a five-day excursion to the Grand Canyon where no one at the Mellowhorn Home had ever been. Twelve people signed up despite the hefty fee to pay for lodging and transportation.

"You only live once!" cried Powder Face.

The group included newcomer Church Bollinger and Forrie Wintka, a.k.a. Theresa Worley, a.k.a. Terry Dolan and, finally, as Terry Taylor. Forrie and Bollinger sat together in the van, had drinks together in the bar of El Tovar, ate dinner at a table for two and planned a trail-ride expedition for the next morning. But before the mule train left, Forrie asked Bollinger to take some photographs she could send to her granddaughters. She stood on the parapet with the famous view behind her. She posed with one hand holding her floppy new straw hat purchased in the hotel gift shop. She took off the hat and turned, shading her eyes with her hand, and pretended to be peering into the depths like a stage character of yore. She clowned, pretending she was unsteady and losing her balance. There was a stifled "Oh!" and she disappeared. A park ranger rushed to the parapet and saw her on the slope ten feet below, clutching at a small plant. Her hat lay to one side. Even as he climbed over the parapet and reached for her, the plant trembled and loosened. Forrie dug her fingers into the gravel as she began to slide toward the edge. The ranger thrust his foot toward her, shouting for her to grab on. But his saving kick connected with Forrie's hand. She shot down the slope as one on a waterslide, leaving ten deep grooves to mark her trail, then, in a last desperate effort, reached for and almost seized her new straw hat.

The subdued group returned to Wyoming the next day. Again and again they told each other that she had not even cried out as she fell, something they believed denoted strong character.

*   *   *

Ray Forkenbrock resumed his memoir the next weekend. Berenice waited a few minutes after Beth arrived before taking up a listening post outside the room. Mr. Forkenbrock had a monotonous but loud voice, and she could hear every word.

"So, things was better for the family after he got the jobs driving machine parts around to the oil rigs," he said. "The money was pretty good and he joined some one of them fraternal organizations, the Pathfinders. And they had a ladies' auxiliary, which my mother got into; they called it 'The Ladies,' like it was a restroom or something. They both got real caught up in Pathfinders, the ceremonies, the lodge, the good deeds and oaths of allegiance to whatever.

"Mother was always baking something for them," he said. "And there was kid stuff for us, fishing derbies and picnics and sack races. It was like Boy Scouts, or so they said. Boy Scouts with a ranch twist, because there was always some class in hackamore braiding or raising a calf. Sort of a kind of a mix of Scouts and 4-H which we did not belong to."

Berenice found this all rather boring. When would he say something about the Bledsoes? She saw Deb Slaver at the far end of the hall coming out of Mr. Harrell's room with a tray of bandages. Mr. Harrell had a sore on his shin that wouldn't heal and the dressing had to be changed twice a day.

"Now don't you pick at it, you bad boy!" yelled Deb, disappearing around the corner.

"Anyway, Mother was probably more into it than Dad. She liked company and hadn't had much luck with neighbors there in Coalie Town. The Ladies got up a program of history tours to various massacre sites and old logging flumes. Mother loved those trips. She had a little taste for what had happened in the

21

long ago. She'd come home all excited and carrying a pretty rock. She had about a dozen rocks from those trips when she died," he said.

In the hall Berenice thought of her sister toiling up rocky slopes, trying to please her rock hound husband, carrying his canvas sack of stones.

"The first hint I got that there was something peculiar in our family tree was when she come home from a visit to Farson. I do not know what they were doing there, and she said that the Farson Auxiliary had served them lunch—potato salad and hot dogs," he said.

"One of the Farson ladies said she knew a Forkenbrock down in Dixon. She thought he had a ranch in the Snake River valley. Well, my ears perked up when I heard 'ranch,'" he said.

"And Forkenbrock ain't that common of a name. So I asked Mother if they were Dad's relatives," he said. "I would of liked it if we had ranch kin. I was already thinking about getting into cowboy ways. She said no, that Dad was an orphan, that it was just a coincidence. So she said."

At dinner that night, once Forrie Wintka's dramatic demise had been hashed through again, Church Bollinger began to describe his travels through the Canadian Rockies.

"What we'd do is fly, then rent a car instead of driving. Those interstates will kill you. The wife enjoyed staying at nice hotels. So we flew to San Francisco and decided to drive down the coast. We stopped in Hollywood. Figured we'd see what Hollywood was all about. They had these big concrete columns. Time came to leave, I got in and backed up and crunch, couldn't get out. I finally got out but I had a bad scratched door on the rental car. Well, I bought some paint and I painted it and you could never tell.

I drove to San Diego. Waited for a letter from the rental outfit but it never came. Another time I rented a car there was a crack in the windshield. I says, 'Is this a safety problem?' The guy looks at me and says 'No.' I drive off and it never *was* a problem. We did the same thing when we went to Europe. In Spain we went to the bullfights. We left after two. I wanted to experience that."

"But are they wounded?" asked Powder Face.

Mr. Bollinger, thinking of rental cars, did not reply.

When Berenice told Chad Grills about old Mr. Forkenbrock who used to work for his grandparents, he was interested and said he would talk to them about it next time he went out to the ranch. He said he hoped Berenice liked ranch life because he was in line to inherit the place. He told Berenice to find out all she could about Forkenbrock's working days. Some of those cagey old boys managed to get themselves situated to put a claim on a ranch through trumped-up charges of unpaid back wages. Whenever Beth came with her tape recorder, Berenice found something to do in the hall outside Ray Forkenbrock's room, listening, expecting him to tell about the nice ranch he secretly owned. She didn't know what Chad would do.

Ray said, "I think when she heard about the Dixon Forkenbrocks, Mother had a little feeling that something wasn't right because she wrote back to the Farson lady thanking her for the nice lunch. I think she wanted to strike up a friendship so she could find out more about the Dixon people, but, far as I know, that didn't happen. It stuck in my mind that we wasn't the only Forkenbrock family." Beth was glad he didn't pause so often now that he was into the story, letting his life unreel.

"The last day of school was a trip and a big picnic. The whole outfit usually went on the picnic, since learning academies of the day was small and scattered. When I was twelve the seventh grade had only three kids—me, one of my sisters who skipped a grade and Dutchy Green. We was excited when we found out the trip was to the old Butch Cassidy outlaw cabin down near the Colorado border. Mrs. Ratus, the teacher, got the map of Wyoming hung up and showed us where it was. I seen the word 'Dixon' down near the bottom of the map. Dixon! That's where the mystery Forkenbrocks lived. Dutchy was my best friend and I told him all about it and we tried to figure a way to get the bus to stop in Dixon. Maybe there'd be a sign for the Forkenbrock Ranch," he said.

"As it turned out," he said, "we stopped in Dixon anyways because there was something wrong with the bus.

"There was a pretty good service station in Dixon that had been an old blacksmith shop. The forge was still there and the big bellows, which us boys took turns working, pretending we had a horse in the stall. I asked the mechanic who was fixing the bus if he knew of any Forkenbrocks in town and he said he heard of them but didn't know them. He said he had just moved down from Essex. Dutchy and me played blacksmith some more but we never got to Butch Cassidy's cabin because they couldn't fix the bus and another one had to come take us back. We ate the picnic on the bus on the way home. After that I kind of forgot about the Dixon Forkenbrocks," he said. He was beginning to slow down again.

"I didn't think about it until Dad died in an automobile accident on old route 30," he said.

"He was taking a shortcut, driving on the railroad ties, and a train come along," he said.

He said, "I'd been working for the Bledsoes for a year and hadn't been home."

At the mention of the Bledsoes, Berenice, out in the hallway, snapped her head up.

"Mr. Bledsoe drove me back so I could attend the funeral. They had it in Rawlins and the Pathfinders had took care of everything," he said.

Beth looked puzzled. "Pathfinders?"

"That organization they belonged to. Pathfinders. All we had to do with it was show up. Which we done. Preacher, casket, flowers, Pathfinder flags and mottoes, grave plot, headstone—all fixed up by the Pathfinders." He coughed and took a sip of whiskey, thinking of cemetery weeds and beyond the headstones the yellow wild pastures.

Berenice couldn't listen anymore because the chime for Cook's Treats rang. It was part of her job to bring the sweets to the residents, the high point in their day trumped only by the alcoholic Social Hour. Cook was sliding triangles of hot apple pie onto plates.

"You hear about Deb's husband? Had a heart attack while he was hitching the tow bar to some tourist. He's in the hospital. It's pretty serious, touch and go. So we won't be seeing Deb for a little while. Maybe ever. I bet she's got a million insurance on him. If he dies and Deb gets a pile a money, I'm going to take out a policy on my old man."

When Berenice carried out the tray of pie, Mr. Forkenbrock's door stood open and Beth was gone.

Sundays Berenice and Chad Grills drove out on the back roads in Chad's almost-new truck. Going for a ride was their kind of date. The dust was bad, churned up by the fast-moving energy company trucks. Chad got lost because of all the new, unmarked roads the companies had put in. Time after time they turned onto a good road only to end up at a dead-end compression station or well pad. Getting lost where you had been born, brought up and never left was embarrassing, and Chad cursed the gas outfits. Finally he took a sight line on Doty Peak and steered toward it, picking the bad roads as the true way. Always his mind seized on a mountain. In a flinty section they had a flat tire. They came out at last near the ghost town of Dad. Chad said it hadn't been a good ride and she had to agree, though it hadn't been the worst.

Deb Slaver did not come in all the next week, and the extra work fell on Berenice. She hated changing Mr. Harrell's bandage and skipped the chore several times. She was glad when on Wednesday, Doc Nelson's visit day, he said Mr. Harrell had to go into the hospital. On Saturday, Beth's day to visit Mr. Forken-brock, Berenice got through her chores in a hurry so she could lean on a dust mop outside the door and listen. Impossible to know what he'd say next with all the side stories about his mother's garden, long-ago horses, old friends. He hardly ever mentioned the Bledsoes who had been so good to him.

"Grandpa," said Beth. "You look tired. Not sleeping enough? What time do you go to bed?" She handed him the printout of his discourse.

"My age you don't need sleep so much as a rest. Permanent rest. I feel fine," he said. "This looks pretty good—reads easy as a book." He was pleased. "Where did we leave off," he said, turning the pages.

"Your dad's funeral," said Beth.

"Oh boy," he said. "That was the day I think Mother begin to put two and two together. I sort of got it, at least I got it that something ugly had happened, but I didn't really understand until years later. I loved my dad so I didn't want to understand.

I still got a little Buck knife he give me and I wouldn't part with it for anything in this world," he said.

There was a pause while he got up to look for the knife, found it, showed it to Beth and carefully put it away in his top drawer.

"So there we all were, filing out of the church on our way to the cars that take us to the graveyard, me holding Mother's arm, when some lady calls out, "Mrs. Forkenbrock! Oh, Mrs. Forken-brock!" Mother turns around and we see this big fat lady in black with a wilted lilac pinned on her coat heading for us," he said.

"But she sails right past, goes over to a thin, homely woman with a boy around my age and offers her condolences. And then she says, looking at the kid, 'Oh, Ray, you'll have to be the man of the house now and help your mother every way you can,'" he said. He paused to pour into the whiskey glass.

"I want you to think about that, Beth," he said. "You are so strong on family ties. I want you to imagine that you are at your father's funeral with your mother and sisters and somebody calls your mother, then walks right over to another person. And that other person has a kid with her and that kid has your name. I was—all I could think was that they had to be the Dixon Forken-brocks and that they was related to us after all. Mother didn't say a word, but I could feel her arm jerk," he said. He illustrated this by jerking his own elbow.

"At the cemetery I went over to the kid with my name and asked him if they lived in Dixon and if they had a ranch and was they related to my father who we was burying. He gives me a look and says they don't have a ranch, they don't live in Dixon but in LaBarge, and that it is *his* father we are burying. I was so mixed up at this point that I just said 'You're crazy!' and went back to Mother's side. She never mentioned the incident and finally we went home and got along like usual although with damn little money. Mother got work cooking at the Sump ranch. It was only when she died in 1975 that I put the pieces together," he said. "All the pieces."

On Sunday Berenice and Chad went for their weekly ride. Berenice brought her new digital camera. For some reason Chad insisted on going back to the tangle of energy roads, and it was almost the same as before—a spiderweb of wrong-turn gravel roads without signs. Far ahead of them they could see trucks at the side of the road. There was a deep ditch with black pipe in it big enough for a dog to stroll through. They came around a corner and men were feeding a section of pipe into a massive machine that welded the sections together. Berenice thought the machine was interesting and put her camera up. Behind the machine a truck idled, a grubby kid in dark glasses behind the wheel. Thirty feet away another man was filling in the ditch with a backhoe. Chad put his window down, grinned and, in an easy voice, asked the kid how the machine worked.

The kid looked at Berenice's camera. "What the fuck do you care?" he said. "What are you doin out here anyway?"

"County road," said Chad, flaring up, "and I live in this county. I was born here. I got more rights to be on this road than you do."

The kid gave a nasty laugh. "Hey, I don't care if you was born on top of a flagpole, you got *no* rights interferin with this work and takin pictures."

"Interfering?" But before he could say any more the man inside the pipe machine got out and the two who had been handling the pipe walked over. The backhoe driver jumped down. They all looked salty and in good shape. "Hell," said Chad, "we're just out for a Sunday ride. Didn't expect to see anybody working on Sunday. Thought it was just us ranch types got to do

28

that. Have a good day," and he trod on the accelerator, peeling out in a burst of dust. Gravel pinged the undercarriage.

Berenice started to say "What was *that* all about?" but Chad snapped "Shut up" and drove too fast until they got to the black-top and then he floored it, looking in the rearview all the way. They didn't speak until they were back at Berenice's. Chad got out and walked around the truck, looking it over.

"Chad, how come you to let them throw off on you like that?" said Berenice.

"Berenice," he said carefully, "I guess that you didn't see one a them guys had a .44 on him and he was taking it out of the hol-ster. It is not a good idea to have a fight on the edge of a ditch with five roustabouts in a remote area. Loser goes in the ditch and the backhoe guy puts in five more minutes of work. Take a look at this," he said, and he pulled her around to the back of the truck. There was a hole in the tailgate.

"That's Buddy's .44 done that," he said. "Good thing the road was rough. I could be dead and you could still be out there entertaining them." Berenice shuddered. "Probably," said Chad, "they thought we were some kind of environmentalists. That camera of yours. Leave it home next time."

Right then Berenice began to cool toward Chad. He seemed less manly. And she would take her camera wherever she wanted.

On Monday Berenice was in the kitchen looking for the ice cream freezer which hadn't been used for two years. Mr. Mel-lowhorn had just come back from Jackson with a recipe for apple pie ice cream and he was anxious for everyone to share his delight. As she fumbled in the dark cupboard Deb Slaver banged in, bumping the cupboard door.

"Ow!" said Berenice.

"Serves you right," snarled Deb, sweeping out again. There was a sound in the hall as of someone kicking a stuffed dog.

"She's pretty mad," said Cook. "Duck didn't die so she don't get the million-dollar insurance, but even worse, he's going to need dedicated care for the rest of his life—hand and foot waiting on, nice smooth pillows. She's got to take care of him forever. I don't know if she'll keep working and try to get an aide to come in or what. Or maybe Mr. Mellowhorn will let him stay here. Then we'll *all* get to wait on him hand and foot."

Saturday came, and out of habit, because she had broken up with Chad and no longer really cared about the Bledsoes or their ranch, Berenice hung around in the hall outside Mr. Forkenbrock's room. Beth had brought him a dish of chocolate pudding. He said it was good but not as good as whiskey and she poured out his usual glass.

"So," said Beth. "At the funeral you met the other Forkenbrocks but they didn't live in Dixon anymore?"

"No. No, no," he said. "You ain't heard a thing. The ones at the funeral were *not* the Dixon Forkenbrocks. They was the LaBarge Forkenbrocks. There was another set in Dixon. When Mother died, me and my sisters had a go through her stuff and sort it all out," he said.

"I'm sorry," said Beth. "I guess I misunderstood."

"She had collected all Dad's obituaries she could find. She never said a word to us. Kept them in a big envelope marked 'Our Family.' I never knew if she meant that sarcastic or not. The usual stuff about how he was born in Nebraska, worked for Union Pacific, then for Ohio Oil and this company and that, how he was a loyal Pathfinder. One said he was survived by Lottie Forkenbrock and six children in Chadron, Nebraska. The boy was named Ray. Another said his grieving family lived in Dixon, Wyoming, and included his wife Sarah-Louise and two sons, Ray and Roger. Then there was one from the Casper *Star* said he was a well-known Pathfinder survived by wife Alice, sons Ray and Roger, daughters Irene and Daisy. That was us. The last one said his wife was Nancy up in LaBarge and the kids were Daisy, Ray and Irene. That was four sets. What he done, see, was give all the kids the same names so he wouldn't get mixed up and say 'Fred' when it was Ray."

He was breathless, his voice high and tremulous. "How my mother felt about this surprise he give her I never knew because she didn't say a word," he said.

He swallowed his whiskey in a gulp and coughed violently, ending with a retching sound. He mopped tears from his eyes. "My sisters bawled their eyes out when they read those death notices and they cursed him, but when they went back home they never said anything," he said. "Everybody, the ones in LaBarge and Dixon and Chadron and god knows where else kept real quiet. He got away with it. Until now. I think I'll have another whiskey. All this talking kind of dries my throat," he said, and he got the bottle himself.

"Well," said Beth, trying to make amends for misunderstanding, "at least we've got this extended family now. It's exciting finding out about all the cousins."

"Beth, they are not cousins. Think about it," he said. He had thought she was smart. She wasn't.

"Honestly, I think it's cool. We could all get together for Thanksgiving. Or Fourth of July."

Ray Forkenbrock's shoulders sagged. Time was swinging down like a tire on the end of a rope, slowing, letting the old cat die.

"Grandfather," said Beth gently. "You have to learn to love your relatives."

He said nothing, and then, "I loved my father.

"That's the only one I loved," he said, knowing it was hopeless, that she was not smart and she didn't understand any of what he'd said, that the book he thought he was dictating would be regarded as an old man's senile rubbish. Unbidden, as wind shear hurls a plane down, the memory of the old betrayal broke the prison of his rage and he damned them all, pushed the tape recorder away and told Beth she had better go back home to her husband.

"It's ridiculous," Beth said to Kevin. "He got all worked up about his father who died back in the 1930s. You'd think there would have been closure by now."

"You'd think," said Kevin, his face seeming to twitch in the alternating dim and dazzle of the television set.

I've Always Loved
This Place

Duane Fork, the Devil's demon secretary, rushed around readying the suite of offices. He sprinkled grit and dust on the desktops, gravel on the floor, pulled closed the heavy red velvet drapes and sprayed the room with Eau de Fumier. Precisely on the dot of midnight he heard the familiar hoof steps coming down the hallway and drew up to attention.

"Good morning, sir," said Duane obsequiously.

"Merde," grunted the Devil, looking around with a peevish eye. "This place is—unspeakable." He had just come back from the Whole World Design & Garden show in Milan, where he posed as an avant-garden-furniture designer who worked in crushed white paper. "If it gets rain-spotted and grimy, who cares? Just kick it into the barbecue and burn it up," he advised. But all the while his guts were twisting with jealous desire as he looked at plastic poolside sofas, walkways beneath pleached tree boughs, tropical palm gardens, rock grottoes and cantilevered decks. On the way back to Hell he leafed through half a dozen design glossies, filled out the subscription blank for *Dwell* and thought briefly of starting a rival publication to be called *Dwell in Hell*. Studying the magazines, he understood that his need was more for landscaping, riverside parks and monuments than for architectural design.

"Nothing has been done with this damn place for aeons. It's old-fashioned, it's passé, people yawn when they think of Hell. Slimy rocks and gloomy forests do not have the negative frisson of yesteryear—there are environmentalists now who love such features. We need to keep up with the times. Modernize. Expand and enlarge. We've *got* to enlarge now that our Climate Rehab Program is working—deserts, melting glaciers, inundations. We're starting to look frumpy in comparison. And, Duane, all signs in the Human Abode point to a major religious war on the way; if we don't get ready for an influx we'll have a vexing problem."

On the way home from the design show he had also read a japish piece in a screed that called itself *The Onion* pretending to report on the addition of a tenth circle to accommodate an increasing number of Total Bastards, most of them American businessmen. The Devil had smiled. A tenth circle was not a bad idea, but Hell's coming population increase would demand much more than providing quarters for tobacco lobbyists and corporate executives. In the long run there was probably no need to build an extension; since nearly all humans were inevitably damned, a simple inversion would do, much like turning a length of intestine inside out and using it as a sausage casing. The earth itself, with no labor on his part, would become Hell Plus. In the meantime he intended to upgrade the current facilities.

"Today, Duane, we are going to tour the property and see where we can make improvements. I want you to bring your notebook. *Andiamo!*" They set out on a red golf cart, the Devil wearing only his shooting jacket, Duane, an eyeshade.

On the way the Devil tossed out infomercial nuggets he had absorbed from his study of the magazines. "It's not so much that we want to tear things down and start over with restructuring, bulldozers, topsoil and fill and imported rocks. What we want is to see the potential in what's already here and work with that. The basic bones of the place are good. We know that. We'll use a construction outfit that has worked in Iraq—Rout & Massacre sounds like our kind of company. Give them a call and get an idea of their fees. If they are too high we'll forcibly transfer them here and make them a local company."

At the main gate the Devil rolled his eyes.

"Got to keep the sign," he said. "You can't really improve on that last line, 'ABANDON HOPE, ALL YE WHO ENTER HERE!' But the gate is boring. Without the sign it's just another Romanesque stone gate. But if we replace it with something modern like the St. Louis arch and an electric fall—"

Duane Fork's furrowed brow and wry face indicated confusion.

"What's the matter?" asked the Devil. "You prefer pepper spray?"

"Oh no! I guess I just don't know what an electric fall is."

"Heard of a waterfall, haven't you?"

"Yessir."

"An electric fall is the same thing, but with electricity, not water. Of course we could mix them—that make you happy?"

"I'm happy with whatever you want to do, sir."

"Good. Make a note. Entrance Gate—St. Louis arch with electrified waterfall."

At the river the Devil cracked a few jokes with Charon but had no suggestions for enhancing the crossing process after the old man snarled "Fine just the way it is." Charon's hot-coal eyes winked spasmodically. He smote five or six naked wretches with his oar and said, "You remember to pick up my eyedrops?"

"Damn!" said the Devil. "I forgot again! Next time for sure. Try sticking your head in the river." He floored it and they drove away from the riverbank, whizzed through the suburb of Limbo.

"Bor-ring," said the Devil, glancing at the writers and poets standing around the film producers, the scribblers holding manuscripts and talking up their ideas.

At the second circle, the source of the dark-and-stormy-night literary genre and a warehouse for marital cheaters, the Devil bawled, "Close the wind vent, Minos, it's wrecking my coif." As they drove he switched on the golf cart's headlight and recognized a few of the adulterous spirits maledict. "How they hangin, baby?" he said, slapping Paris on the rump. Duane Fork dared to lick Cleopatra's left breast. Ideas for reshaping this corner of Hell did not come; it was cast in stone that adulterers would puke and heave in permanent nausea; it would be a waste of time to design anything more than the concrete gutters already in situ.

It was not until the third circle that the Devil came alive with inventive eagerness. Cold rain and sleet hammered down on soil the consistency of a decayed sponge. Figures writhed in the mud. The Devil paused to hear some of the latest gossip which came in a hundred languages. The hoarse, desperate howling of Cerberus echoed from the black cliffs.

"Bad boy! Bad boy!" shouted the Devil encouragingly as he tossed the creature a handful of meatballs. Multiple heads snapped at the flying treats, none escaping the triple throat. Cerberus barked out thanks and a bit of news.

"Did you know that about Sarkozy?"

"No sir," said Duane, taking a note.

"We can do something here," said the Devil. "What we need are all those things that made New Orleans so great—slippery car tops, floating boards with protruding nails, a lot of sewage in the water, conflicting orders. Or maybe a tsunami once in a while. The place seems made for a classy tsunami. And I would like a heavy miasma to hang over everything. This ground fog is almost worthless." He looked at the Stygian rock slopes streaming with black water. "Hell, the view alone is worth billions. Breathtaking. I've always loved this place."

The golf cart lurched through the mire. They skirted the great marsh that prefaced the river Styx, but the sounds of the damned choking on silty mud carried through the humid atmosphere like hundreds of hogs at the trough. On the far shore they could see an unbelievably steep mountain and on its peak the city of Dis outlined against a fiery sky. At the boat landing the Devil whistled shrilly, and in the distance they saw the boatman Phlegyas poling toward them.

"You know, this is really Charon's job, but I put him on the Acheron because he's got a maître d' personality—ushers in the newcomers with style. And Phlegyas is good enough at what he does." The powerful boatman lifted the golf cart into the vessel and they set out across black water crowded with floundering swimmers whose numbers impeded the boat's progress.

"Take a note, Duane. We want to put two or three hundred saltwater crocs in here. Order them from Australia. Double our fly-gnat-mosquito-chigger package order."

Once landed at the base of the mountain, the Devil made a frame with his fingers and held it up against various vistas. He kept coming back to the city at the top.

"Location, location," he murmured. "And we've been wasting it all this time. It is the ideal end point for the Tour de France. Pro cyclists have earned a place in Hell. It is twice the size of any Alp." They set off up the steep slope, swerving around the boulders on the path.

"Just what I thought. Soft and easy. Let's take a page from the Paris-Roubaix race, erroneously called 'the Hell of the North.' Let's get some coarse and broken cobbles on the steepest stretches here. I want those guardrails removed from the abyss, and plenty of flints and Clovis points protruding from the final five kilometers. Varied weather will help; sleet storms, parching heat, black ice on the cobbles, hurricane force crosswinds and a few thousand clones of that German so-called Devil guy who dresses up in a smelly red union suit and runs around with a cardboard pitchfork, the jerk. He's been looking at too many old woodcuts and I've got a place for him some sweet day. Every rider will be on drugs and some will go down frothing at the lips like Simpson on Mount Ventoux in nineteen sixty-whatever. And let's have screaming crowds who throw buckets of filth and fine dust, handfuls of carpet tacks, who squirt olive oil and then piss on the riders. Water bottles filled with kerosene or alkali water. Riders have to fix their own bikes and carry spare tires around their necks. If they fall off and break an arm or leg no one can help them. More dogs on the course. And rattlesnakes. Let's see—how about an obligatory enema in the starting gate and EPO breaks every thirty minutes? As for the UCI—" He whispered in the demon's ear.

"*Chapeau!*" cried Duane Fork.

At the city of Dis the Devil told the enraged and tormented inhabitants to get ready for big-time bicycle racing. Gliding down through the next circles the Devil decided on a number of presidential suites modeled on Japanese hotel cubicles and Wal-Mart men's rooms, added a slaughterhouse nightclub and made the decision that after a newcomer passed through the gate and was discharged by Charon into the main Welcome to Hell foyer he or she would find combined features of the world's worst air terminals, Hongqiao in Shanghai the ideal, complete with petty officials, sadomasochistic staffers, consecutive security checks of increasing harshness, rapidly fluctuating gate changes and departure times and, finally, a twenty-seven-hour trip in an antiquated and overcrowded bucket flying through typhoons while rivets popped against the fuselage.

On the climb up to Dis the Devil had noticed a cluster of

scorched bowlegged men lollygagging near a boiling water hole. This area was posted as a reserve for Italian Renaissance politicians. Trespassing was forbidden.

"I'll be damned," he said. "That's Butch Cassidy and some of his old gang. Cheeky bastards. Let's plan something good for all the old rustlers and cowboys who have made it over the winding trail. I think we'll give them a taste of their own medicine. Let's get the Four Horsemen and some of our assistant imp riders and start herding those cowboys into bunches, cutting them out and moving them into pens. We'll rope and throw them, castrate, vaccinate and brand them with my big Pitchfork iron. Oh, there'll be plenty of dust and bawling and pleas. They'll try to break away. They will screech and gibber. In the end we'll turn them in to a sand pasture full of cheatgrass, goat-heads, cockleburs and ticks. They can ride the bicycles discarded by the tour racers and listen to Slim Whitman doing 'Indian Love Call' over the loudspeaker."

"Ranchers, too?" asked Duane Fork.

"Nah. Nothing here would bother *them*." He thought a moment and then said, "Wait! Better yet, give the ranchers herds of irritable minotaurs. And headstrong centaurs for mounts. Which reminds me, order one roasted for my dinner."

"Which, minotaur, centaur or ranchaur?"

"Whatever's easiest. Medium rare."

As they drew abreast of the loungers the Devil called, "Hey, Butch, fucked any mules lately? Ha ha ha ha. Shake that wooden leg."

Annoyed by the polyglot babbling of Dis, the Devil decided to standardize. "I think we'll make the Khoisan language of the Bushmen the official language of Hell," he said in a fluent stipple of dental, palatal, alveolar, lateral and bilabial clicks. Duane Fork whooshed agreement.

"Your accent is getting better, Duane, but it is still not crisp enough." The Devil looked around at the mud and black trona-water fountains. "I don't see any nettles or leafy spurge or mille-foil or crabgrass or water hyacinth. Let's get a few of those USDA hacks to work—get some devil's club in here."

The Devil's thoughts kept turning back to bicycle racers and he called the guard tower and ordered all the Junior Satan Scouts who patrolled the approach to the city to helpfully point racers toward projecting street furniture, pylons, potholes and drop-offs. Now that he was tuned in to something he was mentally calling "Sports of Hell," the ideas flew like lekking mayflies. Duane Fork's pencil ripped across the pages, skidding at the end of each line. Soccer alone sprouted eleven hundred improve-ments, and from soccer it was an easy leap to cricket and caber tossing and on to special arrangements for rental chefs, insecticide manufacturers, world leaders, snowplow drivers.

"Construction workers!" the Devil shouted. "Their hard hats will melt, their scaffolds collapse unceasingly. Ice cream truck vendors? A hot coal in each scoop of vanilla. Goat turds in the chocolate—I'll make them myself." He seized two fire cones from the roadside dispenser for refreshment. Then a glimpse of roasting moneylenders in the distance made him think of banks and loans, bills and taxes.

"Canada Revenue! We'll let them play hockey, their national sport, down on Circle Nine's ice."

"Wouldn't the IRS be better? More infamous?"

"Duane, the IRS is a babe in the woods compared to Canada Revenue. There is no agency on earth as contumacious, bureau-cratized, power-obsessed, backhanded, gouging, red-taped, cav-ernous and carnivorous as Canada Revenue."

"But if hockey is their national sport, won't they take pleasure in playing it?"

I'VE ALWAYS LOVED THIS PLACE

"I think not. The blades will be inside the skates. And those blades will be warm."

But the idea of a tenth circle haunted him. He might do it. It would have to be something utterly unexpected, a stunning surprise, a coup. As he steered the golf cart it came to him—an art museum. Not just a collection of works earthly museum directors wished to consign to Hell but depictions of himself through the millennia in every guise from monstrous yellow-eyed goats to satin-winged bats, the fabulous compartments of the Nether Regions and, of course, a catalog of human vices and evils, of plummeting sinners.

His ideas tumbled out. In one of the museum's galleries he would set up the Musical Inferno which Hieronymus Bosch had painted so cleverly. He would have all of Goya's witches and his stinking hordes, toothless, pierced, howling, wracked and terrified. He would have every piece of Satanic art even though many showed him as humbled by upward-gazing saints; he always had the last laugh there. Venusti showed a fatuous Saint Bernard holding him chained, but a moment later the chain had melted. The painter had not dared to show that. Michael Pacher had given him a fabulous frog-green skin, but the deer antlers and the buttocks-face were overdone. Gerard David's portrait was finer. A special room for Gustave Doré, whose inventiveness he cherished. Very pleasant as well were the many harvest pictures where he tossed damned souls into his fireproof gunnysack. He would crowd the museum with all the Last Judgments, the damned dropping into the inferno like ripe figs from a tree. Signorelli—he couldn't understand how Signorelli had known to give his demons green and grey and violet skins—a lucky guess perhaps. And surely one of Signorelli's demons was Duane Fork biting at a man's head? He might ask the painter—

if he could find him. They had to start compiling a database of the damned and their particular niches; it was impossible to find anyone in Hell.

Still on the idea of the art museum, he planned a solitary room with no other paintings where he thought he would hang William Blake's *Satan Instigating the Rebel Angels,* which showed him as the most beautiful angel of all, more handsome than any Greek god, before the rebellion failed and he was cast down and out. But thinking of that time made him morose and he decided to eschew the Blake; he'd have Rubens instead and Tiepolo. As he made his mental list of the paintings and sculptures he intended to gather, he realized what a terrific labor it would be to pry them away from the Prado, the Duomo, the Louvre, the Beaux-Arts, various art institutes and bibliothèques, private collections and monasteries, cathedrals and churches. The plan abruptly crashed. Well, well, there was the rub; he was not going into any monasteries or churches. And there the renovation plans stopped. His one-track mind could not get past the monasteries, cathedrals and churches.

He ought to have plucked some professional art thieves from their fiery labors and sent them up to do the job, but the story says nothing about that.

Them Old Cowboy Songs

There is a belief that pioneers came into the country, home-
steaded, lived tough, raised a shoeless brood and founded ranch
dynasties. Some did. But many more had short runs and were
quickly forgotten.

ARCHIE & ROSE, 1885

Archie and Rose McLaverty staked out a homestead where the Little Weed comes rattling down from the Sierra Madre, water
named not for miniature and obnoxious flora but for P. H. Weed,
a gold seeker who had starved near its source. Archie had a face as
smooth as a skinned aspen, his lips barely incised on the surface as
though scratched in with a knife. All his natural decoration was in
his red cheeks and the springy waves of auburn hair that seemed
charged with voltage. He usually lied about his age to anyone who
asked—he was not twenty-one but sixteen. The first summer they
lived in a tent while Archie worked on a small cabin. It took him
a month of rounding up stray cows for Bunk Peck before he could
afford two glass windows. The cabin was snug, built with eight-

foot squared-off logs tenoned on the ends and dropped into mortised uprights, a size Archie could handle with a little help from their only neighbor, Tom Ackler, a leathery prospector with a summer shack up on the mountain. They chinked the cabin with heavy yellow clay. One day Archie dragged a huge flat stone to the house for their doorstep. It was pleasant to sit in the cool of the evening with their feet on the great stone and watch the deer come down to drink and, just before darkness, to see the herons flying upstream, their color matching the sky so closely they might have been eyes of wind. Archie dug into the side of the hill and built a stout meat house, sawed wood while Rose split kindling until they had four cords stacked high against the cabin, almost to the eaves, the pile immediately tenanted by a weasel.

"He'll keep the mice down," said Rose.

"Yeah, if the bastard don't bite somebody," said Archie, flexing his right forefinger. "And you'll wear them windows out, warshin em so much," but he liked the way the south glass caught Barrel Mountain in its frame. A faint brogue flavored his sentences, for he had been conceived in Ireland, born in 1868 in Dakota Territory of parents arrived from Bantry Bay, his father to spike ties for the Union Pacific Railroad. His mother's death from cholera when he was seven was followed a few weeks later by that of his father, who had whole-hog guzzled an entire bottle of strychnine-laced patent medicine guaranteed to ward off cholera and measles if taken in teaspoon quantities. Before his mother died she had taught him dozens of old songs and the rudiments of music structure by painting a plank with black and white piano keys, sitting him before it and encouraging him to touch the keys with the correct fingers. She sang the single notes he touched in her tone-pure voice. The family wipeout removed the Irish influence. Mrs. Sarah Peck, a warmhearted Missouri Methodist widow, raised the young orphan to the great resentment of her son, Bunk.

*   *   *

A parade of saddle bums drifted through the Peck bunkhouse and from an early age Archie listened to the songs they sang. He was a quick study for a tune, had a memory for rhymes, verses and intonations. When Mrs. Peck went to the land of no breakfast forever, caught in a grass conflagration she started while singeing slaughtered chickens, Archie was fourteen and Bunk in his early twenties. Without Mrs. Peck as buffer, the relationship became one of hired hand and boss. There had never been any sense of kinship, fictive or otherwise, between them. Especially did Bunk Peck burn over the hundred dollars his mother left Archie in her will.

Everyone in the sparsely settled country was noted for some salty dog quirk or talent. Chay Sump had a way with the Utes, and it was to him people went when they needed fine tanned hides. Lightning Willy, after incessant practice, shot both pistol and carbine accurately from the waist, seemingly without aiming. Bible Bob possessed a nose for gold on the strength of his discovery of promising color high on the slope of Singlebit Peak. And Archie McLaverty had a singing voice that once heard was never forgotten. It was a straight, hard voice, the words falling out halfway between a shout and a song. Sad and flat and without ornamentation, it expressed things felt but unsayable. He sang plain and square-cut, "Brandy's brandy, any way you mix it, a Texian's a Texian any way you fix it," and the listeners laughed at the droll way he rolled out "fix it," the words surely meaning castration. And when he moved into "The Old North Trail," laconic and a little hoarse, people got set for half an hour of the true history they all knew as he made his way through countless verses. He could sing every song—"Go Long Blue Dog," and "When the Green Grass Comes," "Don't Pull off My Boots," and "Two Quarts of Whiskey," and at all-male roundup nights he had endless verses of "The Stinkin Cow," "The Buckskin Shirt" and "Cousin Harry." He courted Rose singing "never marry no good-for-nothin boy," the boy understood to be himself, the "good-for-nothin" a disclaimer. Later, with winks and innuendo, he sang, "Little girl, for safety you better get branded . . ."

Archie, advised by an ex-homesteader working for Bunk Peck, used his inheritance from Mrs. Peck to buy eighty acres of private land. It would have cost nothing if they had filed for a homestead twice that size on public land, or eight times larger on desert land, but Archie feared the government would discover he was a minor, nor did he want a five-year burden of obligatory cultivation and irrigation. Since he had never expected anything from Mrs. Peck, buying the land with the surprise legacy seemed like getting it for free. And it was immediately theirs with no strings attached. Archie, thrilled to be a landowner, told Rose he had to sing the metes and bounds. He started on the southwest corner and headed east. It was something he reckoned had to be done. Rose walked along with him at the beginning and even tried to sing with him but got out of breath from walking so fast and singing at the same time. Nor did she know the words to many of his songs. Archie kept going. It took him hours. Late in the afternoon he was on the west line, drawing near and still singing though his voice was raspy, "an we'll go downtown, an we'll buy some shirts . . .," and slouching down the slope the last hundred feet in the evening dusk so worn of voice she could hardly hear him breathily half-chant "never had a nickel and I don't give a shit."

There is no happiness like that of a young couple in a little house they have built themselves in a place of beauty and solitude. Archie had hammered together a table with sapling legs and two benches. At the evening meal, their faces lit by the yellow shine of the coal oil lamp whose light threw wild shadows on the ceiling, their world seemed in order until moths flew at the lamp and finally thrashed themselves to sticky death on the plates.

Rose was not pretty, but warmhearted and quick to laugh. She had grown up at the Jackrabbit stage station, the daughter of kettle-bellied Sundown Mealor, who dreamed of plunging steeds but because of his bottle habit drove a freight wagon. The station was on a north-south trail connecting hardscrabble ranches with the blowout railroad town of Rawlins after the Union Pacific line went through. Rose's mother was grey with some wasting disease that kept her to her bed, sinking slowly out of life. She wept over Rose's early marriage but gave her a family treasure, a large silver spoon that had come across the Atlantic.

The stationmaster was the politically minded Robert F. Dorgan, affable and jowly, yearning to be appointed to a position of impor tance and seeing the station as a brief stop not only for freight wagons but for himself. His second wife, Flora, stepmother to his daughter, Queeda, went to Denver every winter with Queeda, and so they became authorities on fashion and style. They were as close as a natural mother and daughter. In Denver, Mrs. Dorgan sought out important people who could help her husband climb to success. Many political men spent the winter in Denver, and one of them, Rufus Clatter, with connections to Washington, hinted there was a chance for Dorgan to be appointed as territorial surveyor.

"I'm sure he knows a good deal about surveying," he said with a wink.

"Considerable," she said, thinking that Dorgan could find some stripling surveyor to do the work for a few dollars.

"I'll see what I can do," said Clatter, pressing heavily against her thigh, but tensed to step back if she took offense. She allowed him a few seconds, smiled and turned away.

"Should such an appointment come to pass, you will find me grateful."

In the spring, back at the station, where her rings and metallic dress trim cast a golden aura, she bossed the local gossip saying that Archie Laverty had ruined Rose, precipitating their youthful marriage, Rose barely fourteen, but what could you expect from a girl with a drunkard father, an uncontrolled girl who'd had the run of the station, sassing rough drivers and exchanging low repartee with bumpkin cowhands, among them Archie Laverty, a lowlife who sang vulgar songs. She whisked her hands together as though ridding them of filth.

The other inhabitant of the station was an old bachelor—the country was rich in bachelors—Harp Daft, the telegraph key operator. His face and neck formed a visor of scars, moles, wens, boils and acne. One leg was shorter than the other and his voice twanged with catarrh. His window faced the Dorgan house, and a black circle which Rose knew to be a telescope sometimes showed in it.

Rose both admired and despised Queeda Dorgan. She greedily took in every detail of the beautiful dresses, the fire opal brooch, satin shoes and saucy hats so exquisitely out of place at the dusty station, but she knew that Miss Dainty had to wash out her bloody menstrual rags like every woman, although she tried to hide them by hanging them on the line at night or inside pillow slips. Beneath the silk skirts she too had to put up with sopping pads torn from old sheets, the crusted edges chafing her thighs and pulling at the pubic hairs. At those times of the month the animal smell seeped through Queeda's perfumed defenses. Rose saw Mrs. Dorgan as an iron-boned two-faced enemy, the public sweetness offset by private coarseness. She had seen the woman spit on the ground like a drover, had seen her scratch her crotch on the corner of the table when she thought

no one was looking. In her belief that she was a superior creature, Mrs. Dorgan never spoke to the Mealors or to the despica-
ble bachelor pawing his telegraph key, or, as he said, seeking out
constellations.

Every morning in the little cabin Rose braided her straight brown
hair, dabbed it with drops of lilac water from the blue bottle
Archie had presented her on the day of their wedding and wound
it around her head in a coronet, the way Queeda Dorgan bound
up her hair. At night she let it fall loose, releasing the fragrance.
She did not want to become like a homestead woman, skunky
armpits and greasy hair yanked into a bun. Archie had crimpy
auburn locks, and she hoped that their children would get those
waves and his red-cheeked handsome face. She trimmed his hair
with a pair of embroidery scissors dropped in the dust by some
stagecoach lady passenger at the station years before, the silver
handles in the shape of bent-necked cranes. But it was hard,
keeping clean. Queeda Dorgan, for example, had little to do at the
station but primp and wash and flounce, but Rose, in her cabin,
lifted heavy kettles, split kindling, baked bread, scrubbed pots and
hacked the stone-filled ground for a garden, hauled water when
Archie was not there. They were lucky their first winter that the
river did not freeze. Her personal wash and the dishes and floor
took four daily buckets of water lugged up from the Little Weed,
each trip disturbing the ducks who favored the nearby setback for
their business meetings. She tried to keep Archie clean as well. He
rode in from days of chasing Peck's cows or running wild horses
on the desert, stubbled face, mosquito-bitten neck and grimed
hands, cut, cracked nails and stinking feet. She pulled off his boots
and washed his feet in the enamel dishpan, patting them dry
with a clean feed sack towel.

"If you had stockins, it wouldn't be so bad," she said. "If I could get me some knittin needles and yarn I could make stockins."

"Mrs. Peck made some. Once. Took about a hour before they was holed. No point to it and they clamber around in your boots. Hell with stockins."

Supper was venison hash or a platter of fried sage hen she had shot, rose-hip jelly and fresh bread, but not beans, which Archie said had been and still were the main provender at Peck's. Occasionally neighbor Tom Ackler rode down for supper, sometimes with his yellow cat, Gold Dust, riding behind him on the saddle. While Tom talked, Gold Dust set to work to claw the weasel out of the woodpile. Rose liked the black-eyed, balding prospector and asked him about the gold earring in his left ear.

"Used a sail the world, girlie. That's my port ear and that ring tells them as knows that I been east round Cape Horn. And if you been east, you been west, first. Been all over the world." He had a rich collection of stories of storms, violent williwaws and southerly busters, of waterspouts and whales leaping like trout, icebergs and doldrums and enmeshing seaweed, of wild times in distant ports.

"How come you to leave the sailor-boy life?" asked Rose.

"No way to get rich, girlie. And this fella wanted a snug harbor after the pitchin deck."

Archie asked about maritime songs, and the next visit Tom Ackler brought his concertina with him and for hours sea chanteys and sailors' verses filled the cabin, Archie asking for a repeat of some and often chiming in after a single hearing.

> They say old man your horse will die.
> And they say so, and they hope so.
> O poor old man your horse will die.
> O poor old man.

Rose was an eager lover when Archie called "put your ass up like a whippoorwill," and an expert at shifting his occasional glum moods into pleased laughter. She seemed unaware that she lived in a time when love killed women. One summer evening, their bed spread on the floor among the chips and splinters in the half-finished cabin, they fell to kissing. Rose, in some kind of transport began to bite her kisses, lickings and sharp nips along his neck, his shoulder, in the musky crevice between his arm and torso, his nipples until she felt him shaking and looked up to see his eyes closed, tears in his lashes, face contorted in a grimace.

"Oh Archie, I didn't mean to hurt, Archie—"

"You did not," he groaned. "It's. I ain't never been. Loved. I just can't hardly *stand it*—" and he began to blubber "feel like I been shot," pulling her into his arms, rolling half over so that the salty tears and his saliva wet her embroidered waist shirt, calling her his little birdeen, and at that moment she would have walked into a furnace for him.

On the days he was away she would hack at the garden or take his old needle gun and hunt sage grouse. She shot a hawk that was after her three laying hens, plucked and cleaned it and threw it in the soup pot with a handful of wild onions and some pepper. Another day she had gathered two quarts of wild strawberries, her fingers stained deep red that would not wash away.

"Look like you killed and skinned a griz bear by hand," he said. "It could be a bear might come down for his berries, so don't you go pickin no more."

The second winter came on and Bunk Peck laid off all the men, including Archie. Cowhands rode the circuit, moving from ranch to ranch, doing odd jobs in return for a place in the bunkhouse and three squares. Down on the Little Weed, Archie and Rose were ready for the cold. He had waited for good tracking snow and shot two elk and two deer in November when the weather chilled, swapping a share of the meat to Tom Ackler for his help, for it could take a lone man several days to pack a big elk out, with bears, lions and wolves, coyotes, ravens and eagles gorging as much of the unattended carcass as they could. One rough acre was cleared where Archie planned to sow Turkey Red wheat. The meat house was full. They had a barrel of flour and enough baking powder and sugar for the city of Chicago. Some mornings the wind stirred the snow into a scrim that bleached the mountains and made opaline dawn skies. Once the sun below the horizon threw savage red onto the bottom of the cloud that hung over Barrel Mountain and Archie glanced up, saw Rose in the doorway burning an unearthly color in the lurid glow.

By spring both of them were tired of elk and venison, tired of bumping into each other in the little cabin. Rose was pregnant. Her vitality seemed to have ebbed away, her good humor with it. Archie carried her water buckets from the river and swore he would dig a well the coming summer. It was hot in the cabin, the April sun like a furnace door ajar.

"You better get somebody knows about well diggin," she said sourly, slapping the bowls on the table for the everlasting elk stew, nothing more than meat, water and salt simmered to chewability, then reheated for days. "Remember how Mr. Town got killed when his well caved in and him in it?"

"A well can damn cave in and *I* won't be in it," he said. "I got in mind not diggin a deep killin well, but clearin out that little seep east a the meat house. Could make a good spring and I'd build a springhouse, put some shelves, and maybe git a cow. Butter and cream cow. Hell, I'm goin a dig out that spring today." He was short but muscular, and his shoulders had broadened, his chest filled out with the work. He started to sing "got to bring along my shovel if I got a dig a spring," ending with one of Tom's yo-heave-hos, but his jokey song did not soothe her irritation. An older woman would have seen that although they were little more than children, they were shifting out of days of clutching love and into the long haul of married life.

"Cows cost money, specially butter and cream cows. We ain't got enough for a butter dish even. And I'd need a churn. Long as we are dreamin, might as well dream a pig, too, give the skim and have the pork in the fall. Sick a deer meat. It's too bad you spent all your money on this land. Should a saved some out."

"Still think it was the right way to do, but we sure need some chink. I'm ridin to talk with Bunk in a few days, see can I get hired on again." He pulled on his dirty digging pants still spattered with mud from the three-day job of the privy pit. "Don't git me no dinner. I'll dig until noon and come in for coffee. We got coffee yet?"

Bunk Peck took pleasure in saying there was no job for him. Nor was there anything at the other ranches. Eight or ten Texas cowhands left over from last fall's Montana drive had stayed in the country and taken all the work.

He tried to make a joke out of it for Rose, but the way he breathed through his teeth showed it wasn't funny. After a few minutes she said in a low voice, "At the station they used a say they pay a hunderd a month up in Butte."

"Missus McLaverty, I wouldn't work in no mine. You married you a cowboy." And he sang "I'm just a lonesome cowboy who loves a gal named Rose, I don't care if my hat gets wet or if I freeze my toes, but I won't work no copper mine, so put that up your nose." He picked a piece of turnip from the frying pan on the stove and ate it. "I'll ride over Cheyenne way an see what I can find. There's some big ranches over there and they probly need hands. Stop by Tom's place on my way and ask him to look in on you."

The next day he went on the drift. We need the chink, she thought, don't we?

Despite the strong April sun there was still deep snow under the lodgepoles and in north hollows around Tom Ackler's cabin; the place had a deserted feeling to it, something more than if Tom had gone off for the day. His cat, Gold Dust, came purring up onto the steps but when Archie tried to pet her, tore his hand and with flattened ears raced into the pines. Inside the cabin he found the stub of a pencil and wrote a note on the edge of an old newspaper, left it on the table.

> Tom I looking for werk arond Shyanne.
> Check on Rose now & than, ok?
> Arch McLaverty

In a saloon on a Cheyenne street packed with whiskey mills and gambling snaps he heard that a rancher up on Rawhide Creek was looking for spring roundup hands. The whiskey bottles glittered as the swinging doors let in planks of light—Kellogg's Old Bourbon, Squirrel, McBryan's, G. G. Booz, Day Dream and a few sharp-cornered gin bottles. He bought the man a drink. The thing was, said his informant, a big-mustached smiler showing rotten nutcrackers, putting on the sideboards by wrapping his thumb and forefinger around the shot glass to gain another inch of fullness, that although Karok paid well and he didn't hardly lay off men in the fall, he would not hire a married man, claiming they had the bad habit of running off home to see wife and kiddies while Karok's cows fell in mud holes, were victimized by mountain lions and rustlers, drifted down the draw and suffered the hundred other ills that could befall untended cattle. The bartender, half-listening, sucked a draught of Wheatley's Spanish Pain Destroyer from a small bottle near the cash register.

"Stomach," he said to no one, belching.

Big Mustache knocked back his brimming shot of Squirrel and went on. "He's a foreigner from back east, and the only thing counts to him is cows. He learned that fast when he come here back in the early days, cows is the only thing. Grub's pretty poor, too. There ain't no chicken in the chicken soup."

"Yeah, and no horse in the horseradish," said Archie who'd heard all the feeble bunkhouse jokes.

"Huh. Well, he rubs some the wrong way. Most a them quit. What I done. Some law dog come out there once with his hand hoverin over his shooter and I could see he was itchin to dabble in gore. I felt like it was a awful good place a put behind me. But there's a few like Karok's ways. Maybe you are one a them. Men rides for him gets plenty practice night ropin. See, his herd grows like a son of a bitch if you take my meanin. But I'll give you some advice: one a these days there'll be some trouble there. That's how come that law was nosin round."

Archie rode up through country as yellow and flat as an old newspaper and went to see Karok. There was a big sign on the gate: NO MaRIED MeN. When the dour rancher asked him, Archie lied himself single, said that he had to fetch his gear, would be back in six days.

"Five," said the kingpin, looking at him suspiciously. "Other fellas look for work they carry their fixins. They don't have to go home and git it."

Archie worked up some story about visiting Cheyenne and not

knowing he'd been laid off until one of the old outfit's boys showed up and said they were all on the bum and, said Archie, he had come straight to Karok when he heard there might be a job.

"Yeah? Get goin, then. Roundup started two days ago."

Back on the Little Weed with Rose, he half-explained the situation, said she would not be able to send him letters or messages until he worked something out, said he had to get back to Karok's outfit fast and would be gone for months and that she had better get her mother to come down from the station and stay, to help with the baby expected in late September.

"She can't stand a make that trip. You know how sick she is. Won't you come back for the baby?" Even in the few days he had been gone he seemed changed. She touched him and sat very close, waiting for the familiar oneness to lock them together.

"If I can git loose I will. But this is a real good job, good money, fifty-five a month, almost twict what Bunk Peck pays and I'm goin a save ever nickel. And if she can't come down, you better go up there, be around womenfolk. Maybe I can git Tom to bring you up, say in July or August? Or sooner?" He was fidgety, as though he wanted to leave that minute. "He been around? His place was closed up when I stopped there before. I'll stop again on my way."

Rose said that if she had to go to the station early September was soon enough. She did not want to be where she would have to tend her sick mother and put up with her drunk father, to see the telegraph man's face like an eroded cliff, to suffer Mrs. Dorgan's supercilious comments about "some people" directed at Queeda but meant for Rose to hear, did not want to show rough and distended beside Queeda's fine dresses and slenderness, to appear abandoned, without the husband they had prophesied would skedaddle. September was five months away and she would worry about it when it came. Together they added up what a year's pay might come to working for Karok.

"If you save everthing it will be six hundred fifty dollars. We'll be rich, won't we?" she asked in a mournful tone he chose not to notice.

He spoke enthusiastically. "And that's not countin what I maybe can pick up in wolf bounties. Possible another hunderd. Enough to git us started. I'm thinkin horses, raise horses. Folks always need horses. I'll quit this feller's ranch after a year an git back here."

"How do I get news to you—about the baby?"

"I don't know yet. But I'll work somethin out. You know what? I feel like I need my hair combed some. You want a comb my hair?"

"Yes," she said, and laughed just when he'd thought she was going to cry. But for the first time she recognized that they were not two cleaving halves of one person but two separate people, and that because he was a man he could leave any time he wanted, and because she was a woman she could not. The cabin reeked of desertion and betrayal.

ARCHIE & SINK

Men raised from infancy with horses could identify salient differences with a glance, but some had a keener talent for understanding equine temperament than others. Sink Gartrell was one of those, the polar opposite of Montana bronc-buster Wally Finch, who used a secret ghost cord and made unrideable outlaws of the horses he was breaking. Sink gave off a hard air of competence. On roundup the elegant Brit remittance man Morton Frewen had once noticed him handling a nervous cloud-watcher horse and remarked that the rider had "divine hands." The adjective set the cowhands guffawing and imitating Frewen's stuffed-nose accent for a few days, but ridicule slid off Sink Gartrell like water off a river rock.

Sink thought the new kid might make a top hand with horses if he got over being a show-off. The second or third morning after he joined the roundup Archie had wakened early, sat up in his bedroll while cookie Hel was stoking his fire, and let loose a getting-up holler decorated with some rattlesnake yodels, startling old Hel, who dropped the coffeepot in the fire, and earning curses from the scattered bedrolls. The black smell of scorched coffee knocked the day over on the wrong side. Foreman Alonzo Lago, who had barely noticed him before, stared hard at the curly-haired new hand who'd made all the noise. Sink noticed him looking.

Later Sink took the kid aside and put the boo on him, told him the facts of life, said that old Lon would bull him good if ever he agreed to get into a bedroll with him, said that the leathery old foreman was well known for bareback riding of new young hires. Archie, who'd seen it all at Peck's bunkhouse, gave him a look as though he suspected Sink of the same base design, said he could take care of himself and that if anyone tried anything on him he'd clean his plow good. He moved off. When Sink came in from watch at the past-midnight hour, he walked past the foreman's bedroll but there was only a solitary head sticking out from under the tarpaulin; the kid was somewhere far away in the sage with the coyotes. Just the same, thought Sink, he would watch Lon the next time he got into the red disturbance and starting spouting that damn poem about Italian music in Dakota, for the top screw was a sure-enough twister.

For Archie the work was the usual ranch hand's luck—hard,

dirty, long and dull. There was no time for anything but saddle up, ride, rope, cut, herd, unsaddle, eat, sleep and do it again. On the clear, dry nights coyote voices seemed to emanate from single points in straight lines, the calls crisscrossing like taut wires. When cloud cover moved in, the howls spread out in a different geometry, overlapping like concentric circles from a handful of pebbles thrown into water. But most often the wind surging over the plain sanded the cries into a kind of coyote dust fractioned into particles of sound. He longed to be back on his own sweet place fencing his horse pastures, happy with Rose. He thought about the coming child, imagined a boy half-grown and helping him build wild horse traps in the desert, capturing the mustangs. He could not quite conjure up a baby.

As the late summer folded Sink saw that Archie sat straight up in the saddle, was quiet and even-tempered, good with horses. The kid was one of the kind horses liked, calm and steady. No more morning hollers and the only songs he sang were after supper when somebody else started one, where his voice was appreciated but never mentioned. He kept to himself pretty much, often staring into the distance, but every man had something of value beyond the horizon. Despite his ease with horses he'd been bucked off an oily bronc ruined beyond redemption by Wally Finch, and instinctively putting out one hand to break his fall, snapped his wrist, spent weeks with his arm strapped to his body, rode and did everything else one-handed. Foreman Alonzo Lago fired Wally Finch, refused to pay him for ruined horses, even if they were mustangs from the wild herds, sent him walking north to Montana.

"Kid, there's a way you fall so's you don't get hurt," said Sink. "Fold your arms, see, get one shoulder up and your head down. You give a little twist while you're fallin so's you hit the ground with your shoulder and you just roll right on over and onto your feet." He didn't know why he was telling him this and grouched up. "Hell, figure it out yourself."

ROSE & THE COYOTES

July was hot, the air vibrating, the dry land like a scraped sheep hoof. The sun drew the color from everything and the Little Weed trickled through dull stones. In a month even that trickle would be dried by the hot river rocks, the grass parched white and preachers praying for rain. Rose could not sleep in the cabin, which was as hot as the inside of a black hatbox. Once she carried her pillow to the big stone doorstep and lay on its chill until mosquitoes drove her back inside.

She woke one morning exhausted and sweaty and went down to the Little Weed hoping for night-cooled water. There was a dark cloud to the south and she was glad to hear the distant rumble of thunder. In anticipation she set out the big kettle and two buckets to catch rainwater. The advance wind came in, thrashing tree branches and ripping leaves. The grass went sidewise. Lightning danced on the crest of Barrel Mountain, and then a burst of hail swallowed up the landscape in a chattering, roaring sweep. She ran inside and watched the ice pellets flail the river rocks and slowly give way to thrumming rain. The rocks disappeared in the foam of rising water. Almost as quickly as it had started the rain stopped, a few last hailstones fell and against the moving cloud the arc of a double rainbow promised everything. Her buckets were full of sweet water and floating hailstones. She stripped and poured dippers of goose-bump water over her head again and again until one bucket was nearly empty and she was shaking. The air was as cool and fresh as September, the heat broken. Around midnight the rain began again, slow and steady. Half awake she could hear it dripping on the stone doorstep.

The next morning it was cold and sleety and her back ached; she wished for the heat of summer to return. She staggered when she walked and it didn't seem worthwhile to make coffee. She drank water and stared at the icy spicules sliding down the window glass. Around midmorning the backache increased, working itself into a slow rhythm. It dawned on her very slowly that the baby was not waiting for September. By afternoon the backache was an encircling python and she could do nothing but pant and whimper, the steady rattle of rain dampening her moaning call for succor. She wriggled out of her heavy dress and put on her oldest nightgown. The pain increased to waves of cramping agony that left her gasping for breath, on and on, the day fading into night, the rain torn away by wind, the dark choking hours eternal. Another dawn came sticky with the return of heat and still her raw loins could not deliver the child. On the fourth afternoon, voiceless from calling for Archie, her mother, Tom Ackler, Tom Ackler's cat, from screaming imprecations at all of them, at god, any god, then at the river ducks and the weasel, to any entity that might hear, the python relaxed its grip and slid off the bloody bed, leaving her spiraling down in plum-colored mist.

It seemed late afternoon. She was glued to the bed and at the slightest movement felt a hot surge that she knew was blood. She got up on her elbows and saw the clotted child, stiff and grey, the barley-rope cord and the afterbirth. She did not weep but, filled with an ancient rage, got away from the tiny corpse, knelt on the floor ignoring the hot blood seeping from her and rolled the infant up in the stiffening sheet. It was a bulky mass, and she felt the loss of the sheet as another tragedy. When she tried to stand the blood poured, but she was driven to bury the child, to end the horror of the event. She crept to the cupboard, got a dish towel and rewrapped him in a smaller bundle. Her hand closed on the silver spoon, her mother's wedding present, and she thrust it into the placket neck of her nightgown, the cool metal like balm.

Clenching the knot of the dish towel in her teeth, she crawled out the door and toward the sandy soil near the river, where, still on hands and knees, still spouting blood, she dug a shallow hole with the silver spoon and laid the child in it, heaping it with sand and piling on whatever river stones were within reach. It took more than an hour to follow her blood trail back to the cabin, the twilight deep by the time she reached the doorstep.

The bloody sheet lay bunched on the floor and the bare mattress showed a black stain like the map of South America. She lay on the floor, for the bed was miles away, a cliff only birds could reach. Everything seemed to swell and shrink, the twitching bed leg, a dank clout swooning over the edge of the dishpan, the wall itself bulging forward, the chair flying viciously—all pulsing with the rhythm of her hot pumping blood. Barrel Mountain, bringing darkness, squashed its bulk against the window and owls crashed through, wings like iron bars. Struggling through the syrup of subconsciousness in the last hour she heard the coyotes outside and knew what they were doing.

As the September nights cooled, Archie got nervous, went into town as often as he could, called at the post office, but no one saw him come out with any letters or packages. Alonzo Lago sent Sink and Archie to check some distant draws ostensibly for old renegade cows too wily or a few mavericks too young to be caught in any roundup.

"What's eatin you?" said Sink as they rode out, but the kid shook his head. Half an hour later he opened his mouth as if he were going to say something, looked away from Sink and gave a half shrug.

"Got somethin you want a say," said Sink. "Chrissake say it. I got my head on backwards or what? You didn't know we was goin a smudge brands? Goin a get all holy about it, are you?"

Archie looked around.

"I'm married," he said. "She is havin a baby. Pretty soon."

"Well, I'm damned. How old are you?"

"Seventeen. Old enough to do what's got a be did. Anyway, how old are *you*?"

"Thirty-two. Old enough a be your daddy." There was a half-hour silence, then Sink started again. "You know old Karok don't keep married fellers. Finds out, he'll fire you."

"He ain't goin a find out from me. And it's more money than I can git on the Little Weed. But I got a find a way Rose can let me know. About things."

"Well, I ain't no wet nurse."

"I know that."

"Long as you know it." Damn fool kid, he thought, his life already too complicated to live, and said aloud, "Me, I wouldn't never git hitched to no fell-on-a-hatchet female."

The next week half the crew went in to town and Archie spent an hour on the bench outside the post office writing on some brown wrapping paper, addressed the tortured missive to Rose at the stage station where he believed her to be. What about the baby, he wrote. Is he born? But inside the post office the walleyed clerk with fingernails like yellow chisels told him the postage had gone up.

"First time in a hunderd year. Cost you two cents a send a letter now," he smirked with satisfaction. Archie, who had only one cent, tore up his letter and threw the pieces in the street. The wind dealt them to the prairie, its chill promising a tight-clenched winter.

*   *   *

Rose's parents, the Mealors, moved to Omaha in November seeking a cure for Mrs. Mealor's declining health.

"You think you can stay sober long enough to ride down and let Rosie and Archie know we are going?" the sick woman whispered to Sundown.

"Why I am goin right now soon as I find my other boot. Just you don't worry, I got it covered."

A full bottle of whiskey took him as far as the river crossing. Dazedly drunk, he rode to the little cabin on the river but found the place silent, the door closed. Swaying, feeling the landscape slide around, he called out three or four times but was unable to get off his horse and knew well enough that if he did he could never get back on.

"G'up! Home!" he said to Old Slope and the horse turned around.

"They're not there," he reported to his wife. "Not there."

"Where could they be? Did you put a note on the table?"

"Didn't think of it. Anyway, not there."

"I'll write her from Omaha," she whispered.

Within a week of their departure a replacement freighter arrived, Buck Roy, his heavyset wife and a raft of children. The Mealors, who had failed even to be buried in the stage station's cemetery, were forgotten.

There were no cattle as bad as Karok's to stray, and ranchers said it was a curious thing the way his cows turned up in distant locations. December was miserable, one storm after another bouncing in like a handful of hurled poker chips, and January turned cold enough to freeze flying birds dead. Foreman Alonzo

Lago sent Archie out alone to gather any bovine wanderers he could find in a certain washout area, swampy in June, but now hundreds of deep holes and snaky little streams smoothly covered with snow.

"Keep your eyes peeled for any Wing-Cross leather-pounders. Better take some sticks and a cinch ring." So Archie knew he was looking for Wing-Cross cows to doctor their brands. But the Wing-Cross had its own little ways with brand reworkings, so he guessed it was more or less an even exchange.

The horse did not want to go into the swamp maze. It was one of the warm days between storms and the snow was soft. Archie dismounted and led his horse, keeping to the edge of the bog, waded through wet snow for hours. The exercise sweated him up. Only two cows allowed themselves to be driven out into the open, the others scattering far back into the coyote willows behind the swamp. In the murky, half-frozen world of stream slop and trampled stems there was no way a man alone could fix brands. He watched the cows circle around to the backcountry. The wind dived, pulling cold air with it. The weather was changing. When he reached the bunkhouse four hours after dark, the thermometer had fallen to zero. His boots were frozen, and, chilled to the liver, he fell asleep without eating or undressing beyond his boots.

"Git back and git them cows," hissed Alonzo Lago two hours later, leaning over his face. "Git up and on it. Rat now! Mr. Karok wants them cows."

"Goddamn short nights on this goddamn ranch," muttered Archie, pulling on his wet boots.

Back in the swamp it was just coming light, like grey polish on the cold world, the air so still Archie could see the tiny breath cloud of a finch on a willow twig. Beneath the hardened crust the snow was wallowy. His fresh horse was Poco, who did not know swamps. Poco blundered along, stumbled in an invisible sinkhole and took Archie deep with him. The snow shot down his neck, up his sleeves, into his boots, filled eyes, ears, nose, matted his hair. Poco, in getting up, rammed his hat deep into the bog. The snow in contact with his body heat melted, and as he climbed back into the saddle the wind that accompanied the pale sunlight froze his clothes. Somehow he managed to push eight Wing-Cross strays out of the swamp and back toward the high ground, but his matches would not light and while he struggled to make a fire the cows scattered. He could barely move and when he got back to the bunkhouse he was frozen into the saddle and had to be pried off the horse by two men. He heard cloth rip.

Sink thought the kid had plenty of sand, and muttering that he wasn't no wet nurse, pulled off the icy boots, unbuttoned coat and shirt, half-hauled him stumbling to his bunk and brought two hot rocks from under the stove to warm him up. John Tank, a Texas drifter, said he had an extra pair of overalls Archie could have—old and mended but still with some wear in them.

"Hell, better'n ridin around bare-ass in January."

But the next morning when Archie tried to get up he was overcome by dizziness. Boiling heat surged through him, his cheeks flamed red, his hands burned with high fever and he had a dry, constant cough. His head ached, the bunkhouse slopped back and forth as if on rockers. He could not stand, and he breathed with a sound like a blacksmith's bellows.

Sink looked at him and thought, pneumonia. "You look pretty bad. I'll go see what Karok says."

When he came back half an hour later Archie was burning.

"Karok says to git you out a here, but the bastard won't let me take the wagon. He says he's got a cancer in his leg and he needs that wagon for hisself to have the doc at the fort cut it out. Lon's fixin up a kind a travois. His ma had some Indan kin so he knows how to fix it. Sometimes he ain't so bad. We'll git you down to Cheyenne and you can ride the train a where your mother is, your folks, Rawlins, whatever. Karok says. And he says you are fired. I had a tell him you was married so he would let you loose. He was all set a have you die in the bunkhouse. We'll get a doc, beat this down. It's only pneumony. I had it twice."

Archie tried to say his mother was long gone and that he needed to get to Rose down on the Little Weed, tried to say that it was sixty-odd miles from Rawlins to their cabin, but he couldn't get out a word because of the wheezing, breath-sucking cough. Sink shook his head, got some biscuits and bacon from the cook.

Foreman Alonzo had trimmed out two long poles and laced a steer hide to them in a kind of sling arrangement. Sink wrapped the legs of a horse named Preacher in burlap to keep the crust from cutting them, lashed the travois poles to his saddle, a tricky business to get the balance right. The small ends projected beyond the horse's ears, but the foreman said that was to accommodate wear on the drag-ends. They rolled Archie and his bedroll in a buffalo robe and Sink began to drag him to Cheyenne, a hundred miles south. With the wagon it would have been easy. Sink thought the travois was not as good a contraption as Indians claimed. The wind, which had dropped a little overnight, came up, pushing a lofty bank of cloud. After four hours they had covered nine miles. The snow began, increasing in intensity until they were traveling blind.

"Kid, I can't see nothin," called Sink. He stopped and dismounted, went to Archie. The earlier snow had melted as fast as it touched that red, feverish face, but gradually, just a fraction of an inch above the surface of the hot flesh, a mask of ice now formed a grey glaze. Sink thought the mask could become the true visage.

"Better hole up. There's a line shack somewheres around here could we find it. I was there all summer couple years back. Down a little from the top of a hogback."

The horse, Preacher, had also spent that summer at the line camp and he went straight to it now. It was on the lee side of the hogback, a little below the crest. The wind had dumped an immense amount of snow on the tiny cabin, but Sink found the door to the lean-to entryway, and that would do to shelter the horse. A shovel with a broken handle leaned against the side of the single stall. Inside the cabin there was a table and backless chair, a plank bunk about twenty inches wide. The stove was heaped with snow, and the stovepipe lay on the floor. Sink recognized the chipped enamel plate and cup on the table.

He wrestled Archie inside and got him and the buffalo robe onto the plank bunk, then put the stovepipe together and jammed it up through the roof hole. Neither inside nor in the entryway could he see any chunk wood, but he remembered where the old chip pile had been and, using the broken shovel, scraped up enough snow-welded chips to get the fire going. While the chips were steaming and sizzling in the stove, he unsaddled Preacher, removed the gunnysacks from his legs and rubbed the horse down. He checked the lean-to's shallow loft hoping for hay, but there was nothing.

"Goddamn," he said and tore some of the loft floorboards loose to burn in the stove. Back outside he dug through the snow with the broken shovel until he hit ground, got out his knife and sawed off the sun-cured grass until he had two or three hatfuls.

"Best I can do, Preacher," he said, tossing it down for the horse.

It was almost warm inside the shack. From his saddlebag he took a small handful of the coffee beans he always carried. The old coffee grinder was still on the wall but a mouse had built a nest in it, and he had no way to unbolt the machine to clean it out. Unwilling to drink boiled mouse shit, he crushed the beans on the table with the flat of his knife. He looked around for the coffeepot that belonged to the cabin but did not see it. There was a five-gallon coal oil tin near the bunk. He sniffed at it, but could detect no noisome odors, packed it with snow and put it on the stove to melt. It was while he was scraping up snow outside that the edge of the coal oil can hit the coffeepot, which, for some unfathomable reason, had been tossed into the front yard. That too he packed with snow. It looked to him as though the last occupant of the shack had been someone with a grudge, showing his hatred of Karok by throwing coffeepots and burning all the wood. Maybe a Wing-Cross rider.

The coffee was hot and black but when he brought the cup to Archie the kid swallowed one mouthful, then coughed and finally puked it up. Sink drank the rest himself and ate one of the biscuits.

It was a bad night. The bunk was too narrow and the kid so hot and twitchy that Sink swooned in and out of forty-wink snaps of sleep, finally got up and slept in the chair with his head on the table. A serious blizzard and fatal cold began to slide down from the Canadian plains that night, and when it broke twelve days later the herds were decimated, cows packed ten deep against barbwire fences, pronghorn congealed into statues, trains stalled for three weeks by forty-foot drifts and two cowpunchers in a line shack frozen together in a buffalo robe.

It was May before Tom Ackler rode up from Taos where he had spent the fall and winter. Despite the beating sunshine the snow was still deep around his cabin. Patches of bare ground showed bright green with a host of thrusting thistles. He wondered if

Gold Dust had made it through. He could see no cat tracks. He lit a fire using an old newspaper on the table, and just before the flame swallowed it, glimpsed a few penciled words and the signature "Arch McLaverty."

"Lost whatever it was. I'll go down tomorrow and see how they are doin." And he unpacked his saddlebags, wrestled his blankets out of the sack hanging from a rafter where they were safe from mice.

In the morning Gold Dust pranced out of the trees, her coat thick. Tom let her in, threw her a choice piece of bacon.

"Look like you kept pretty good," he said. But the cat sniffed at the bacon, went to the door and, when he opened it, returned to the woods. "Probly shacked up with a bobcat," he said, "got the taste for wild meat." Around noon he saddled the horse and headed for the McLaverty cabin.

No smoke rose from the chimney. A slope of snow lay against the woodpile. He noticed that very little wood had been burned. The weasel's tracks were everywhere, and right up into the eaves. Clear enough the weasel had gotten inside. "Damn sight more comfortable than a woodpile." As he squinted at the tracks the weasel suddenly squirted out of a hole in the eaves and looked at him. It was whiter than the rotting snow, and its black-tipped tail twitched. It was the largest, handsomest weasel he had ever seen, shining eyes and a lustrous coat. He thought of his cat and it came to him that wild creatures managed well through the winter. He wondered if Gold Dust could breed with a bobcat and recalled then that Rose had been expecting. "Must be they went to the station." But he opened the door and looked inside, calling "Rose? Archie?" What he found sent him galloping for the stage station.

*　　*　　*

74

At the station everything was in an uproar, all of them standing in the dusty road in front of the Dorgans' house, Mrs. Dorgan crying, Queeda with her mouth agape and Robert F. Dorgan shouting at his wife, accusing her of betraying him with a human wreck. They paid little attention to Tom Ackler when he slid in on his lathered horse calling that Rose McLaverty was raped and murdered and mutilated by Utes, sometime in the winter, god knew when. Only Mrs. Buck Roy, the new freighter's wife, who was terrified of Indians, gave him much attention. The Dorgans continued to scream at each other. The more urgent event to them was the suicide that morning of the old bachelor telegraph operator who had swallowed lye after weeks of scribbling a four-hundred-page letter addressed to Robert Dorgan and outlining his hopeless adoration of Mrs. Dorgan, the wadded pages fulsomely riddled with references to "ivory thighs," "the Adam and Eve dance," "her secret slit" and the like. What Tom Ackler had thought was an old saddle and a pile of grain sacks on the porch was the corpse.

"Where there's smoke there's fire!" bellowed Robert F. Dorgan. "I took you out a that Omaha cathouse and made you a decent woman, give you everthing and here's how you reward me, you drippin bitch! How many times you snuck over there? How many times you took his warty old cock?"

"I never! I didn't! That filthy old brute," sobbed Mrs. Dorgan, suffused with rage that the vile man had fastened his attentions on her, had dared to write down his lascivious thoughts as real events, putting in the details of her pink-threaded camisole, the red mole on her left buttock, and, finally, vomiting black blood all over the telegraph shack and the front porch of the Dorgans' house where he had dragged himself to die, the four-hundred-page bundle of lies stuffed in his shirt. For years she had struggled to make herself into a genteel specimen of womanhood, grateful that Robert F. Dorgan had saved her from economic sexuality and determined to erase that past. Now, if Dorgan forced her away, she would have to go back on the game, for she could think of no other way to make a living. And maybe Queeda, too, whom she'd brought up as a lady! Her sense of personal worth faltered, then flared up as if doused with kerosene.

"Why you dirty old rum-neck," she said in a hoarse voice, "what gives you the idea that you got a right to a beautiful wife and daughter? What gives you the idea we would stay with you? Look at you—you want a be the territory surveyor, but without me and Queeda to talk up the important political men you couldn't catch a cold."

Dorgan knew it was true and gnawed at his untrimmed mustache. He turned and melodramatically strode into his house, slamming the door so hard the report killed mice. Mrs. Dorgan had won and she followed him in for a reconciliation.

Tom Ackler looked at Queeda who was tracing an arc in the dirt with the toe of her kid-leather boot. They heard the rattle of a stove lid inside the house—Mrs. Dorgan making up a fire to warm the parlor and bedroom.

"Rose McLaverty—" he said, but Queeda shrugged. A tongue of wind lapped the dust, creating a miniature whirl as perfect in shape as any tornado snaking down from black clouds that caught up straws, horsehairs, minute mica fragments and a feather. The dust devil collapsed and died. Queeda turned away, walked around the shaded back of the Dorgan house. Tom Ackler stood holding the reins, then remounted and started back, the horse moving in a kind of equine stroll.

On the way he thought of the whiskey in his cupboard, then of Rose and decided he would get drunk that night and bury her the next day. It was the best he could do for her. He thought too that perhaps it hadn't been Utes who killed her but her young husband, berserk and raving, and now fled to distant ports. He remembered the burned newspaper with Archie's message consumed before it could be read and thought it unlikely if Archie had killed his young wife in a frenzy, that he would stop by a neighbor's place and leave a signed note. Unless maybe it was a confession. There was no way to know what had happened. The more he thought about Archie the more he remembered the clear, hard voice and the singing. He thought about Gold Dust's rampant vigor and rich fur, about the sleek weasel at the McLaverty cabin. Some lived and some died, and that's how it was.

He buried Rose in front of the cabin and for a tombstone wrestled the big sandstone rock Archie had hauled in for a doorstep upright. He wanted to chisel her name but put it off until the snows started. It was too late then, time for him to head for Taos.

The following spring as he rode past their cabin he saw that frost heaves had tipped the stone over and that the ridgepole of the roof had broken under a heavy weight of snow. He rode on, singing "when the green grass comes, and the wild rose blooms," one of Archie's songs, wondering if Gold Dust had made it through again.

The Sagebrush Kid

For George Jones

Those who think the Bermuda Triangle disappearances of planes, boats, long-distance swimmers and floating beach balls a unique phenomenon do not know of the inexplicable vanishings along the Red Desert section of Ben Holladay's stagecoach route in the days when Wyoming was a territory.

Historians have it that just after the Civil War Holladay petitioned the U.S. Postal Service, major source of the stage line's income, to let him shift the route fifty miles south to the Overland Trail. He claimed that the northern California–Oregon–Mormon Trail had recently come to feature ferocious and unstoppable Indian attacks that endangered the lives of drivers, passengers, telegraph operators at the stage stops, smiths, hostlers and cooks at the swing stations, even the horses and the expensive red and black Concord coaches (though most of them were actually Red Rupert mud wagons). Along with smoking letters outlining murderous Indian attacks he sent Washington detailed lists of goods and equipment damaged or lost—a Sharp's rifle, flour, horses, harness, doors, fifteen tons of hay, oxen, mules, bulls, grain burned, corn stolen, furniture abused, the station itself along with barn, sheds, telegraph office burned, crockery smashed, windows ditto. No matter that the rifle had been left propped against a privy, had been knocked to the ground by the wind and buried in sand before the owner exited the structure, or that the dishes had disintegrated in a whoop-up shooting contest, or that the stagecoach damage resulted from shivering passengers building a fire inside the stage with the bundles of government documents the coach carried. He knew his bureaucracy. The Washington post office officials, alarmed at the bloodcurdling news, agreed to the route change, saving the Stagecoach King a great deal of money, important at that time while he, privy to insider information, laid his plans to sell the stage line the moment the Union Pacific gathered enough shovels and Irishmen to start construction on the transcontinental railroad.

Yet the Indian attack Holladay so gruesomely described was nothing more than a failed Sioux war party, the battle ruined when only one side turned up. The annoyed Indians, to reap something from the trip, gathered up a coil of copper wire lying on the ground under a telegraph pole where it had been left by a wire stringer eager to get to the saloon. They carted it back to camp, fashioned it into bracelets and necklaces. After a few days of wearing the bijoux, most of the war party broke out in severe rashes, an affliction that persisted until a medicine man, R. Singh, whose presence among the Sioux cannot be detailed here, divined the evil nature of the talking wire and caused the remainder of the coil and all the bracelets and earbobs to be buried. Shortly thereafter, but in no apparent way connected to the route change or the copper wire incident, travelers began to disappear in the vicinity of the Sandy Skull station.

The stationmaster at Sandy Skull was Bill Fur, assisted by his wife, Mizpah. In a shack to one side a telegraph operator banged his message key. The Furs had been married seven years but had no children, a situation in those fecund days that caused them both grief. Mizpah was a little cracked on the subject and traded one of Bill's good shirts to a passing emigrant wagon for a baby pig, which she dressed in swaddling clothes and fed from a nipple-fitted bottle that had once contained Wilfee's Equine Liniment & Spanish Pain Destroyer but now held milk from the Furs' unhappy cow—an object of attention from range bulls, rustlers and roundup cowboys, who spent much of her time hiding in a nearby cave. The piglet one day tripped over the hem of the swaddling dress and was carried off by a golden eagle. Mrs. Fur, bereft, traded another of her husband's shirts to a passing emigrant wagon for a chicken. She did not make the swaddling gown mistake twice, but fitted the chicken with a light leather jerkin and a tiny bonnet. The bonnet acted as blinders and the unfortunate poult never saw the coyote that seized her within the hour.

Mizpah Fur, heartbroken and suffering from loneliness, next fixed her attention on an inanimate clump of sagebrush that at twilight took on the appearance of a child reaching upward as if piteously begging to be lifted from the ground. This sagebrush became the lonely woman's passion. It seemed to her to have an enchanting fragrance reminiscent of pine forests and lemon zest. She surreptitiously brought it a daily dipper of water (mixed with milk) and took pleasure in its growth response, ignoring the fine cactus needles that pierced her worn moccasins with every trip to the beloved *Atriplex*. At first her husband watched from afar, muttering sarcastically, then himself succumbed to the illusion, pulling up all grass and encroaching plants that might steal sustenance from the favored herb. Mizpah tied a red sash around the sagebrush's middle. It seemed more than ever a child stretching its arms up, even when the sun leached the wind-fringed sash to pink and then dirty white.

Time passed, and the sagebrush, nurtured and cosseted as neither piglet nor chicken nor few human infants had ever been— for Mizpah had taken to mixing gravy and meat juice with its water—grew tremendously. At twilight it now looked like a big man hoisting his hands into the air at the command to stick em up. It sparkled festively in winter snow. Travelers noted it as the biggest sagebrush in the lonely stretch of desert between Medicine Bow and Sandy Skull station. It became a landmark for deserting soldiers. Bill Fur, clutching the handle of a potato hoe, hit on the right name when he announced that he guessed he would go out and clear cactus away from the vicinity of their Sagebrush Kid.

About the time that Bill Fur planed a smooth path to and around the Sagebrush Kid, range horses became scarce in the vicinity of the station. The Furs and local ranchers had always been able to gather wild mustangs, and through a few sessions with steel bolts tied to their forelocks, well-planned beatings with a two-by-four and merciless first rides by some youthful buster whose spine hadn't yet been compressed into a solid rod, the horses were deemed ready-broke to haul stagecoaches or carry riders. Now the mustangs seemed to have moved to some other range. Bill Fur blamed it on the drought which had been bad.

"Found a water hole somewheres else," he said.

A party of emigrants camped overnight near the station, and at dawn the captain pounded on the Furs' door demanding to know where their oxen were.

"Want a git started," he said, a man almost invisible under a flop-rimmed hat, cracked spectacles, full beard and a mustache the size of a dead squirrel. His hand was deep in his coat pocket, a bad sign, thought Bill Fur who had seen a few coat-pocket corpses.

"I ain't seen your oxes," he said. "This here's a horse-change station," and he pointed to the corral where two dozen broom-tails stood soaking up the early sun. "We don't have no truck with oxes."

"Them was fine spotted oxen, all six matched," said the captain in a dangerous, low voice.

Bill Fur, curious now, walked with the bearded man to the place the oxen had been turned out the night before. Hoofprints showed where the animals had ranged around eating the sparse bunchgrass. They cast wide and far but could not pick up the oxen trail as the powdery dust changed to bare rock that took no tracks. Later that week the disgruntled emigrant party was forced to buy a mixed lot of oxen from the sutler at Fort Halleck, a businessman who made a practice of buying up worn-out stock for a song, nursing them back to health and then selling them for an opera to those in need.

"Indans probly got your beasts," said the sutler. "They'll bresh out the tracks with a sage branch so's you'd never know but that they growed wings and flapped south."

The telegraph operator at the station made a point of keeping the Sabbath. After his dinner of sage grouse with rose-haw jelly, he strolled out for an afternoon constitutional and never returned to his key. This was serious, and by Wednesday Bill Fur had had to ride into Rawlins and ask for a replacement for "the bible-thumpin, damn old goggle-eyed snappin turtle who run off." The replacement, plucked from a Front Street saloon, was a tough drunk who lit his morning fires with pages from the former operator's bible and ate one pronghorn a week, scorching the meat in a never-washed skillet.

"Leave me have them bones," said Mizpah, who had taken to burying meat scraps and gnawed ribs in the soil near the Sage-brush Kid.

"Help yourself," he said, scraping gristle and hocks onto the newspaper that served as his tablecloth and rolling it up. "Goin a make soup stock, eh?"

Two soldiers from Fort Halleck dined with the Furs and at nightfall slept out in the sagebrush. In the morning their empty bedrolls, partly drifted with fine sand, lay flat, the men's saddles at the heads for pillows, their horse tack looped on the sage. The soldiers themselves were gone, apparently deserters who had taken leave bareback. The wind had erased all signs of their passage. Mizpah Fur made use of the bedrolls, converting them into stylish quilts by appliquéing a pleasing pattern of black stripes and yellow circles onto the coarse fabric.

It may have been a trick of the light or the poor quality window glass, as wavery and distorting as tears, but Mizpah, sloshing her dishrag over the plates and gazing out, thought she saw the sagebrush's arms not raised up but akimbo, as though holding a water divining rod. Worried that some rambunctious buck trying his antlers had broken the branches, she stepped to the door to get a clear look. The arms were upright again and tossing in the wind.

Dr. Frill of Rawlins, on a solitary hunting trip, paused long enough to share a glass of bourbon and the latest town news with Mr. Fur. A week later a group of the doctor's scowling friends rode out inquiring of the medico's whereabouts. Word was getting around that the Sandy Skull station was not the best place to spend the night, and suspicion was gathering around Bill and Mizpah Fur. It would not be the first time a stationmaster had taken advantage of a remote posting. The Furs were watched for signs of opulence. Nothing of Dr. Frill was ever found, although a hat, stuck in the mud of a playa three miles east, might have been his.

A small group of Sioux, including R. Singh, on their way to the Fort Halleck sutler's store to swap hides for tobacco, hung around for an hour one late afternoon asking for coffee and bread which Mizpah supplied. In the early evening as the dusk thickened they resumed their journey. Only Singh made it to the fort, but the shaken Calcutta native could summon neither Sioux nor American nor his native tongue to his lips. He bought two twists of tobacco and through the fluid expression of sign language tagged a spot with a Mormon freight group headed for Salt Lake City.

A dozen outlaws rode past Sandy Skull station on their way to Powder Springs for a big gang hooraw to feature a turkey pull, fried turkey and pies of various flavors as well as the usual floozy contingent and uncountable bottles of Young Possum and other liquids pleasing to men who rode hard and fast on dusty trails. They amused themselves with target practice on the big sagebrush, trying to shoot off its waving arms. Five of them never got past Sandy Skull station. When the Furs, who had been away for the day visiting the Clug ranch, came home they saw the Sagebrush Kid maimed, only one arm, but that still bravely raised as though hailing them. The telegraph operator came out of his shack and said that the outlaws had done the deed and that he had chosen not to confront them, but to bide his time and get revenge later, for he too had developed a proprietorial interest in the Sagebrush Kid. Around that time he put in a request for a transfer to Denver or San Francisco.

Everything changed when the Union Pacific Railroad pushed through, killing off the stagecoach business. Most of the stage station structures disappeared, carted away bodily by ranchers needing outbuildings. Bill and Mizpah Fur were forced to abandon the Sandy Skull station. After tearful farewells to the Sagebrush Kid they moved to Montana, adopted orphan cowboys and ran a boardinghouse.

*   *   *

The decades passed and the Sagebrush Kid continued to grow, though slowly. The old stage road filled in with drift sand and greasewood. A generation later a section of the coast-to-coast Lincoln Highway rolled past. An occasional motorist, mistaking the Sagebrush Kid for a distant shade tree, sometimes approached, swinging a picnic basket. Eventually an interstate highway swallowed the old road and truckers used the towering Sagebrush Kid in the distance as a marker to tell them they were halfway across the state. Although its foliage remained luxuriant and its size enormous, the Kid seemed to stop growing during the interstate era.

Mineral booms and busts surged through Wyoming without affecting the extraordinary shrub in its remote location of difficult access until BelAmerCan Energy, a multinational methane extraction company, found promising indications of gas in the area, applied for and got permits and began drilling. The promise was realized. They were above a vast deposit of coal gas. Workers from out of state rushed to the bonanza. A pipeline had to go in and more workers came. The housing shortage forced men to sleep four to a bed in shifts at the dingy motels forty miles north.

To ease the housing difficulties, the company built a man-camp out in the sagebrush. The entrance road ran close to the Sagebrush Kid. Despite the Kid's size, because it was just a sagebrush, it went unnoticed. There were millions of sagebrush plants—some large, some small. Beside it was a convenient pull-out. The man-camp was a large gaunt building that seemed to erupt from the sand. The cubicles and communal shower rooms, stairs, the beds, the few doors were metal. A spartan kitchen staffed by Mrs. Quirt, the elderly wife of a retired rancher, specialized in bacon, fried eggs, boiled potatoes, store-bought bread and jam and occasionally a stewed chicken. The boss believed the dreary sagebrush steppe and the monotonous diet were responsible for wholesale worker desertion. The head office let him hire a new cook, an ex-driller with a meth habit whose cuisine revolved around canned beans and pickles.

After three weeks Mrs. Quirt was reinstated, presented with a cookbook and a request to try something new. It was a disastrous order. She lit on complex recipes for boeuf bourguignonne, parsnip gnocchi, bananas stuffed with shallots, kale meatballs with veal ice cream. When the necessary ingredients were lacking she did what she had always done on the ranch—substituted what was on hand, as bacon, jam, eggs. After a strange repast featuring canned clams, strawberry Jell-O and stale bread, many men went outside to heave it up in the sage. Not all of them came back and it was generally believed they had hiked forty miles to the hot-bed motel town.

The head office, seeing production, income and profits slump because they could not keep workers on, hired a cook who had worked for an Italian restaurant. The food improved dramatically, but there was still an exodus. The cook ordered exotic ingredients that were delivered by a huge Speedy Food truck. After the driver delivered the cases of sauce and mushrooms, he parked in the shade of the big sagebrush to eat his noontime bologna sandwich, read a chapter of *Ambush on the Pecos Trail* and take a short nap. Three drillers coming in from the day shift noticed the truck idling in the shade. They noticed it again the next morning on the way to the rig. A refrigerator truck, it was still running. A call came three days later from the company asking if their driver had been there. The news that the truck was still in the sagebrush brought state troopers. After noticing spots of blood on the seat and signs of a struggle (a dusty boot print on the inside of the windshield), they began stringing crime-scene tape around the truck and the sagebrush.

"Kellogg, get done with the tape and get out here," called a sergeant to the laggard trooper behind the sagebrush. The thick branches and foliage hid him from view and the tape trailed limply on the ground. Kellogg did not answer. The sergeant walked around to the back of the sagebrush. There was no one there.

"Goddamn it, Kellogg, quit horsin around." He ran to the front of the truck, bent and looked beneath it. He straightened, shaded his eyes and squinted into the shimmering heat. The other two troopers, Bridle and Gloat, stood slack-jawed near their patrol car.

"You see where Kellogg went?"

"Maybe back up to the man-camp? Make a phone call or whatever?"

But Kellogg was not at the man-camp, had not been there.

"Where the hell did he go? *Kellogg!!!*"

Again they all searched the area around the truck, working out farther into the sage, then back toward the truck again. Once more Bridle checked beneath the truck, and this time he saw something lying against the back inner tire. He pulled it out.

"Sergeant Sparkler, I found this." He held out a tiny scrap of torn fabric that perfectly matched his own brown uniform. "I didn't see it before because it's the same color as the dirt." Something brushed the back of his neck and he jumped, slapping it away.

"Damn big sagebrush," he said, looking at it. Deep in the branches he saw a tiny gleam and the letters "OGG."

"Jim, his nameplate's in there!" Sparkler and Gloat came in close, peering into the shadowy interior of the gnarled sagebrush giant. Sergeant Sparkler reached for the metal name tag.

The botanist sprayed insect repellent on his ears, neck and hair. The little black mosquitoes fountained up as he walked toward the tall sagebrush in the distance. It looked as large as a tree and towered over the ocean of lesser sage. Beyond it the abandoned man-camp shimmered in the heat, its window frames warped and crooked. His heart rate increased. Years before he had scoffed at the efforts of botanical explorers searching for the tallest coast red- wood, or the tallest tree in the New Guinea jungle, but at the same time he began looking at sagebrush with the idea of privately tagging the tallest. He had measured some huge specimens of basin big sagebrush near the Killpecker dunes and recorded their heights in the same kind of little black notebook used by Ernest Hemingway and Bruce Chatwin. The tallest reached seven feet six inches. The monster before him certainly beat that by at least a foot.

As he came closer he saw that the ground around it was clear of other plants. He had only a six-foot folding rule in his back- pack, and as he held it up against the huge plant it extended less than half its height. He marked the six-foot level with his eye. He had to move in close to get the next measurement.

"I'm guessing thirteen feet," he said to the folding rule, placing one hand on a muscular and strangely warm branch.

The Sagebrush Kid stands out there still. There are no gas pads, no compression stations near it. No road leads to it. Birds do not sit on its branches. The man-camp, like the old stage station, has dis- appeared. At sunset the great sagebrush holds its arms up against the red sky. Anyone looking in the right direction can see it.

The Great Divide

1920

The black secondhand Essex rattled and throbbed along the frozen dirt road. The sky drooped over the undulating prairie like unrolled bolts of dirty wool, and even inside the car they could smell the coming snow. There was no heater, and Helen, a young woman with walnut-colored hair, was wrapped from her shoulders down in an old-fashioned buffalo robe, the fur worn to the hide in places. At a small cairn of stones her husband, Hi Alcorn, turned left onto a faint track.

"Close now," he said. "Maybe two miles."

"If that storm don't beat us there," she answered in her breathy voice.

"We're okay," he said. "We're A-okay. Headin for our own place. Year from now drivin up we'll be able to see the lighted windows."

Hi's feet worked the pedals, and she saw that the laces of his old worn oxfords were knotted with bits of string. An impasto of yellow mud which had ossified to stucco and then rubbed back into dust on the Essex's floorboards discolored the shoes.

"I don't see any houses," she said. "It's not like what we heard from Mr. Bewley. He said it would be almost a town by now."

"Not yet. I guess this next year we will all build. The ones of us that come late."

There were two sides to the colony, the east side already settled, the west side, where they had bought a homestead, still unformed.

Hi coughed a little from the dust and went on. "Mr. and Mrs. Wash, like us just startin out, and two brothers, Ned and Charlie Volin. They'll be buildin. The Washes was at the picnic." Abruptly he jerked the wheels to the right where a wooden stake, its top painted white, leaned. Fence posts without wire lined toward the west.

"Was Mrs. Wash the one with the strawberry mark on her chin?"

"I guess that was her. I remember something was wrong about her face. Okay, this's it. Southeast corner. We're on our place. Recognize it?"

They had gone out in May, right after their wedding, looking at homestead sites with Mr. Antip Bewley. They bought the land and had returned in the late summer, at Mr. Bewley's invitation, for the Great Divide picnic. By then they were living in a boardinghouse in Craig. Helen made a few dollars a week helping Mrs. Ruffs change the sheets and cook for the boarders. Mrs. Ruffs was a widow who had carried on her husband's freighting business after he died, but found the care of six horses and their heavy harness too much for her. She sold the business, team and wagons, bought a sizable house in Craig and hung out her sign—RUFFS BED & BOARD. Helen hated the job as all the furniture and the spaces behind the wallpaper were infested with bedbugs. They had a peculiar smell, like old beef fat. Hi, of course, had been out to the property many times, measuring, deciding where the house and barn should go, marking his corners and setting fence posts. One man could set posts well enough, but it took two or three to string the wire.

*   *   *

She would not forget the first sight of Mr. Antip Bewley, huge, towering above Hi. His hands were the size of hay forks. His head, hair and skin the color of raw wood, was shaped as though someone had taken a rectangular chunk of twelve-by-twelve and sanded off the corners, leaving a smooth jawline without disguising the blockiness of the shape. The face was indented by two furrowed cheek dimples. But it was when Bewley smiled that the landscape lit up as though a crackle of lightning had traversed it, for his four front teeth, top and bottom, were solid gold, pure as wedding rings.

"Call me Ant," he had said, pumping Hi's hand, then bending over Helen's rough farm girl paw as though to kiss it or the air above it, in courtly but ironic mockery. They all rode in Mr. Bewley's touring car.

Hi, who subscribed to *The Great Divide,* already knew something about Bewley. He had been reading Bewley's stories championing homestead settlements of public land in defiance of the big cattlemen—"range hogs," he called them. On the way out to the platted sites, the big man talked enthusiastically about converting empty rangeland to happy homesteads that would give "the little people" a chance. Helen, sitting between the two men, was conscious of the body heat each gave off. She made up her mind to sit in the back on the return.

Mr. Bewley talked about growing up in Oklahoma, about his career as a prizefighter, as a lawyer, as a prospector in Alaska and how he had returned to Oklahoma out of love for his wife, and he said this with the same courtly irony as when he had bent over Helen's hand, nudging her with his thigh as though in complicity. She shifted slightly toward Hi.

He told them how he had come to Denver to write for *The*

97

Great Divide. He knew and admired Mr. Bonfils, one of the owners of *The Denver Post,* a powerful friend of "the little people." Helen wished he would not refer to the little people so often. She felt it diminished them, for she and Hi were undoubtedly classed among the lowly peasants. It also seemed unfair to Helen that ordinary men—Hi, for example—had great trouble finding an occupation, while Mr. Antip Bewley had enjoyed so many and cast them all to one side.

They spent the day driving from one homestead site to another, horned larks running before them on the roads, flying up only at the last moment. They walked over acres of level ground that seemed much the same to Helen. Around three o'clock they stopped and rested in the shade of the car. Bewley took a dripping basket from the back. Inside were three apples, chunks of melting ice, six bottles of beer and two of sarsaparilla. Bewley and Hi each drank two beers. Helen walked to a draw out of sight of the car to relieve herself, and as she started back she saw the two men were doing the same, standing side by side, separated by a polite distance of eight or ten feet.

"I'll tell you what," said Antip Bewley, speaking to Hi in a confidential tone as though beer and urination had moved them to another level of intimacy, "there's a kind a special site I been saving for some special people, and I think you are the ones. It's got a real valuable feature. Wait'll you see it."

Helen thought the site looked very much the same as the others and stayed in the car, but Bewley led Hi to a small draw where the vegetation appeared different. Birds flew up as they approached it, and the hoofprints of wild horses showed on the damp soil.

"There," said Bewley. "What do you think of *that?*"

That was a wet seep at the head of the little draw, hardly more than a slanting crease in the otherwise level ground. "Nice little spring. Never goes dry. Dig it out, put in a springhouse and you're set for life."

Right then, Helen, watching from the car, saw that Hi decided this was their place. He tossed his head a little as he always did when he had made up his mind about something.

"Didn't you say we was going to have trees?" Her voice was so light she seemed to have inhaled a ribbon of cloud and to float out her words on its gauzy remnants. But her face was pinched and yellow and she kept her hands under the buffalo robe. He thought she had taken on a Chinese look.

"You saw the place last spring. Did you think trees was goin a grow up by now? We got to plant them. I'll plant them. By the gods, first thing I do soon as the ground thaws, I'll get out here with a load of lumber and some trees and rosebushes. That suit you?" There was in his voice some asperity, as though she had asked for a cobblestone drive and a perpetual fountain.

She nodded, wanting to preserve the peace of the day.

His voice mellowed. "All right, then. Come on, get out and I'll show you the best part."

Slowly, for her joints were half-frozen, Helen got out of the car, slapping dust from her sleeves, and walked into the sharp air. She was very cold and she wished she had worn her brown merino wool skirt. She followed Hi's striding legs, both of them hurrying now because the first few flakes of snow were gliding down. Last spring the land had been rich green starred with wildflowers, for Antip Bewley had shrewdly showed them around when the season was most promising. When, in late summer, they came for the picnic, they had stayed on the east side. The landscape there

99

was sere, the grass a dry brown color like a coffee stain, and she was glad they were to live on the flowery west side. Now it resembled a wasteland.

"Cold!" she gasped, fumbling with the neck button of her light jacket and wishing she had brought a woolen scarf, wishing she had a heavy duster or an overcoat.

"Take a look at this," Hi cried in a joyful voice, spreading his arms wide to encompass the two acres he had plowed and disked with the hired help of a Craig farmer. "Just a second disking in the spring and we'll plant. And how about this?" He pointed to the springhouse he had built a few weeks before. He had cleared out the muddy spring, surrounded it with a cedar box, covered the bottom with clean river gravel and water-smoothed stones, then built a small structure to protect it from range horses, livestock and silt-laden wind. He opened the small door and she could see the black water reflect the square of light that had fallen on it.

She grimaced, and he caught the expression.

"What's the matter with it," he said.

"Nothing! It's swell! It's just that the baby kicked," and she put her hand on her belly as actresses did when they wanted to indicate that they were pregnant.

"Well," he said. "That's fine. Isn't it? Isn't it, honey?"

"Yes."

"That's fine, new land, new springhouse, new big house coming, one baby coming. And we'll name him Joe. Joe is a good name for a boy."

"Yes. Or Jim or Frank." This was old ground. She knew his horror of burdensome names, for the three Alcorn brothers, Hiawatha, Hamilcar and Seneca, had suffered, and their names had been abbreviated to Hi, Ham and Sen by the end of each boy's respective first day in school. Helen teased him sometimes,

100

chanting in a low voice such as she thought an Indian reciter would use

> By the shores of Gitche Gumee,
> By the shining Big-Sea-Water,
> Stood the wigwam of Nokomis,
> Wherein dwelt young Hiawatha . . .

"That's not how it goes," he said in a tight voice, for he did not stand teasing, and he took up a tin cup fastened to the cedar spring casing by a strip of rawhide, dipped it full, handed it, dripping, to her.

"You did a lot of work," she said to mollify him.

"You tell em, kid."

She drank the ice-cold water, pure and sweet and with the faintest taste of cedar, and thought, This is our water, *my* water, for her father had given them one hundred dollars toward the place. The war years had been good for farmers. Corn had gone to two dollars a bushel and it seemed wheat prices would keep rising. The money had helped, for every homestead family, Mr. Bewley said, should have two thousand dollars, six cows, three horses. Hi explained to her on the way to the picnic when the established settlers showed off their squash and corn, that the Great Divide Colony was not a setup for people who were flat busted. It was more for people who had a little something and wanted to get back to the land.

Later, in the pushing crowd, he said "all these people"— waving in the direction of the crowd watching the bathing beauty contest—"have some money, so the colony is a surefire success." Helen and Hi had only six hundred dollars and one cow, but Hi was confident they'd make up for it within five years. He had managed to buy three horses, all of them cheap and half-wild as they were fresh off the Red Desert to the northwest.

"I'll have them gentled down pretty quick," he said. But he was not good with horses and after a few months he sold them, using the money for a down payment on a tractor. He was going to plant corn and wheat.

"Pay the tractor off with what we make on the crops," he'd said.

Now, standing shirtsleeved in the freezing autumn wind he remarked, "Quite a few houses already over on the east side. If it wasn't set for snow we could run over there. You could see." He looked at the churning clouds and the sparse flakes whirling down. She shuddered, said nothing.

"Better idea, hustle back to Craig and get warm. We'll hop right in the bed and get warm." He rapidly raised and lowered his eyebrows communicating a coarse intention. This eyebrow wriggling was something she thought nastily comic.

Both of them came from Tabletop, Iowa. Hi's father was a strong-minded farmer, and her own parents, Rolfe and Netitia Short, owned a small dairy farm. She was the middle child of nine. Her brothers were dairy farmers as well, and Helen, who had developed a dislike of milk cows and their endless care, had married, in part, to escape cows. She had married, too, to escape the household's obsession with bird eggs. Every surface of the house bore blown bird eggs which Rolfe Short and his sons collected. They often took long trips to distant places to gather more eggs. Her father's climbing paraphernalia hung from hooks in the milk room, and even there, among the dust and hen feathers, wild bird eggs rolled in small arcs whenever the door opened. Three of her brothers collected eggs as well, and at the dinner table there was no end to the talk of tree-climbing adventures and perilous forays onto cliffs to seize coveted clutches.

The trip back to Craig was terrifying, the storm suddenly upon them, Hi cursing as he wrestled the car along the slippery ruts, losing the track in the flying snow. It took them five hours to cover twenty-two miles and Helen thought it a miracle they had survived. Hi was white and exhausted but he said the Essex was a peach of a car.

She had met Hi, then only a few months home from the Great War, at the funeral of her older brother, Ned. It was a sultry day, unrelieved by breeze or cloud cover. The mourners cooled themselves with little round fans bearing the name of the undertaker, Farrow's Funerals. Hi's brother Sen had been a friend of Ned's and with him on the ill-fated egg-collecting trip. Ned had climbed a hollow tree stub in a black-water swamp to get the egg of a great blue heron while Sen waited in the boat below, and as Ned came even with the nest, the violent bird, defending her egg, had pierced his eye and brain with her beak.

The first thing Hi said to Helen as they walked away from the fresh grave in the sweating company of the mourners was "If they piled up all the birds' eggs in the world in front a me I would turn the other way." That put it flat. Her mother overheard the remark and took it as oblique blame for their son's death. From that moment she disliked Hi.

Hi was nine years older than Helen. In the war he had suffered a whiff of gas and a wound in his right thigh. He came home with a limp, brusquely unwilling to farm with his father and brothers. The family did not know what to make of him, and his father sang in a sarcastic voice the new song that every farmer knew—"How you gonna keep em down on the farm, after they seen Paree?"

But of course he had not gone to Paris.

"I wouldn't give them the satisfaction," he said, as though his refusal to visit the City of Light somehow punished the French, whom he called "the Froggies," in a jocular, insulting tone. Hi's life now seemed to him a valuable gift that must not be wasted when so many had died in French mud for reasons he still did not understand. He knew he had to get away from his family, from Tabletop with its relentless corn and quivering horizon. He wanted a frontier, though it seemed to him that the frontiers had all disappeared in his grandfather's time. He was, without knowing it, searching for a purpose that his spared body might carry out. Helen, nineteen years old and with long wood-brown hair, came into view as an island to the shipwrecked. They would make their own frontier.

Hi was counting on the corn and wheat prices staying up, and when corn dropped to forty-two cents and wheat plunged from three dollars fifty to a dollar, he was stunned.

"I don't understand how it could slide like that," he said, for he had been too busy for many months to read *The Great Divide*. Now Helen pointed out an article warning that wartime demand had ended and that too many farmers, counting on continuing high prices, had overplanted.

"That don't make sense," he said. "There's still the same bunch a people in the world. They got to eat."

Even if the prices had remained steady, they had to face the fact that neither the wheat nor corn had done well. Only the potatoes had thrived, but potatoes were a cheap crop; anyone could grow them. In November of 1921, Hi went back to Iowa to see his father, not out of family sentiment, but to learn how to make potato whiskey.

They had, of course, to visit her family when they were in Iowa. They spent a bare half hour in the dismal house, then fled.

"See you are in the family way again," her mother said coldly, went silent.

"How can they live that way," mourned Helen on the way home. William had taken up egg collecting once more, not to align in rows in cabinets and on tabletops, but to sell to city collectors who did not have the time or location for egg forays. Soon he was making more money than any dairy farmer, such was the longing of fanciers in New York City and Philadelphia for the eggs of bald eagles, meadowlarks and trumpeter swans. His mother had made him move everything associated with eggs out to the old hen-house, now empty, as she would have nothing in the place that brought back memories of poor Ned. Rather than put up with his mother's icy hatred of what he was doing, William began to live in the henhouse himself, ripping the nest boxes off their support planks and throwing down his dirty blankets. Soon he smelled like a chicken, and looked like one, his clothes festooned with stray feathers.

"My poor brother," Helen said and sighed.

"Huh," said Hi. "He's gone simple. Just a dirty gristle-heel chicken lover."

The potato whiskey didn't work out. Hi was the kind of man who couldn't keep something quiet and within six months the revenuers were onto him. He had picked one of the old Indian caves under the ledges as his place of manufacture, throwing out the Indian corpse wrapped in deerskin and beads. He was cooking mash on a day of clouds smeared by thumbs of wind when the sheriff came in. The judge made him an example—six months in jail and a two-hundred-dollar fine. Helen had to borrow from William to pay the fine. She lied to Hi and told him she had raised the money selling the tractor. She had sold the tractor, but got only fifty dollars for it.

After he got out they moved over the state line to Wyoming in a region of steep pointed hills separated by deep gorges. The desert wilderness lay to the west; to the east the Sierra Madre rose like a great black wave. Helen's curly-headed sister Verla and her husband, Fenk Fipps, lived on one of the highest farms. Antip Bewley had showed and sold them the place.

"That man again," said Helen. It seemed to her that Mr. Bewley had manipulated many lives; no doubt he thought of them as the little people and himself as the puppeteer. All the settlers, dreaming the war prices would come again, grew wheat on the tops of the hills. The local ranchers were against them and there were rumors that two families had been burned out while they were up in Rawlins buying supplies. Helen thought it was a hard country with hard people and longed for their old place west of Great Divide although she had been glad to leave it.

1932

The children were making a tremendous racket, jumping on the beds it sounded like, and after a particularly violent crash a dead silence fell, followed by whispering. Helen went to the door and looked in. One of the beds had collapsed at one end and now resembled a cow getting up.

"For pity's sake," she said. "Your father will be here any time and what do you do? Smash up the furniture." She looked wildly around as though for the stick with which she beat them.

"Listen! That's him!" said Mina, eleven years old and big in the same way Hi was big. The twins, Henry and Buster, were nine, slender and on the short side. Hi often teased them about their heights, urging them to eat plenty and put some meat on their bones. Little Riffie was the spoiled baby, the favorite.

They could all hear the chugging of the car engine as it drew near the porch, and then Hi's feet on the steps, the door opening.

The boys raced for him, Henry already asking if he had brought them anything.

"Alls I could get was a roll a Life Savers. You got to share." He held it out on his palm. Buster grabbed it and ran outside, the others snatching at his shirt.

Helen looked at him. He shook his head. "I go in to Sharps, see, and say I heard he wanted a man. He didn't say a word, just pointed to where that big half-wit Church Davis was throwin bags a grain onto a wagon. His way of saying he already hired Church. Makes you blue to know a half-wit gets a job over you."

Helen's stomach ached. What could they do? She didn't understand why the Depression was harming men who wanted to work. There had to be a way to get money.

From the front window Mina could see a throbbing plume of dust laboring up the hill through the heat. She knew it was going to turn in by the way it slowed.

"Ma! There's a car coming."

Helen wiped her hands on her apron, slipped it off and went to the porch door. A heavy sedan crept up the drive. It was so dusty she could not see the color. Kind of maroon, she thought. The vehicle parked under the cottonwood tree in the only piece of shade. The passenger window rolled down and a face appeared.

"Verla!" she cried and rushed down the steps. To the girls she called "It's your aunt Verla!" The girls advanced, mincing across the gravel on bare feet. A half-grown puppy followed, biting at dress hems. Henry and Buster were a mile distant shooting prairie dogs with slingshots. Verla and Fenk stayed in their seats but rolled the windows down. Fenk's tight-jawed face displayed blackheads mixed with stubble. He had a low smile and dark, staring eyes like those of a marionette. Helen knew he beat his children with a strap and that he had slapped Verla around a few times. She shuddered to think of those wooden eyes painted with malice fastening on her sister.

"Out this way and thought we'd see if you was home," whispered Fenk who had something wrong with his voice that threw it in a high womanish register. Whispering suited him better. Fenk generally let Verla do most of the talking. The story was that he had tried to hang himself as a boy and damaged his voice box. "They get awful moody at a certain age," his mother had offered as explanation, but his old father knew it was probably something else on the other edge of the great divide that separated men's and women's knowledge of sexual matters. He had caught the tail of some sniggered comment about coming or maybe going when he went into the metalwork shop, the informal meeting place for local farmers. Ray Gapes, who owned the smithy, had a large coffeepot and some stage of inky java was always on tap for anyone who could drink it.

Helen leaned into the passenger window, her arms on the hot metal, the breeze that moved always around the cottonwood fluttering the hem of her print dress.

"Where did you get the nice car?" she said. The car gave off a variety of ticks and pings as it cooled. The girls came up, Mina folding her arms across her flat chest, Riffie swinging on the door handle, and listened to the women talk. They too wore cotton print dresses but with puff sleeves and Riffie with a small lace-edged collar that Helen had tatted. Their pale legs were like peeled willow sticks.

"Fenk's makin good money catchin horses," said Verla. "That's how come us to visit." She looked, not at her sister, but at Fenk, waiting for him to nod his head.

Hi appeared from behind the house where he had been grubbing up sagebrush. Helen wanted a kitchen garden and getting the soil in shape was work. He stood near Fenk's window.

Verla said, speaking for Fenk, "Fenk wants Hi to throw in with him. The horses bring five or eight dollars and he has been getting good bunches."

Hi shook his head. His work-enlarged hands, crusted with soil, hung by his sides. "Never done it," he said.

Fenk had to speak. He whispered, "It's good work. Some, like them Tolberts, runs them, some drives them into a box canyon, but we been makin night traps around water holes. That way you don't lose so many tryin to get out. You follow me? The money is good. I been workin with Wacky Lipe."

"Wacky Lipe! Hell, he's got a wood leg."

Verla spoke up. "Yes, and it come off the other night. All the horses run out of the trap and now they're wise to it."

Fenk added, pitching his voice down to alto, "He hopped around pretty good, but wasn't no use. Wacky is all try and no luck." He looked at Hi.

But Hi only said he'd think it over. Henry and Buster came in sight, lagging around the edge of the drought-burned wheat field. When they recognized the passengers in the car they began to run, hoping the male cousins had come. They were disappointed and showed it by punching their sisters and running.

"You boys better stop it," said Helen.

Ten days later the old black Essex quit for good. Hi had made a hundred repairs over the years, had repaired the repairs, but now the entire engine had seized and he knew the thing wasn't worth fixing. There was no money for it anyway, and so he had hoofed it to Fenk and Verla's and told Fenk he was in.

"I knew you'd come in," murmured Fenk. "Well, we're layin out a new trap tomorrow. We don't run horses—takes a lot of time and you need a bunch a riders. I'll leave that to the Tolberts. Old Jim there and his seven boys don't even need to talk they know each other's minds so good. Me and Wacky favor a water trap, you follow? Last month we found a spring the hell off in rough country, horse trails comin in from every direction. Hitched the wagon to the new car and hauled out the posts and cable last week and now we got a build the corral and the wings. Hard drivin out there. I about wrecked that car and Verla's pretty mad. There's deep washes and the stones are hell on the tires. I been thinkin about getting a set a them solid tires like the JO runs on their truck. I been thinkin about saw off the ass end and put a bed on her, follow me? I don't suppose you got a ridin horse these days?"

Hi shook his head. "Just Old Bonnet. The kids ride him mostly. He's about a hunderd years old."

"You can use Big Nose and Crabby."

Hi nodded.

It was a rare day, windless, cool and clear. Fenk and Wacky had set up camp about three miles from the spring where they planned to build the water trap. They came to the camp in late afternoon, Fenk's sedan hauling the horse trailer, wallowing across the flats and washes. The country was rough, full of cliffs and arroyos, and Hi liked being out in it. The canvas tent at the foot of a sandstone bluff was stained red with desert dust and crowded inside with bedrolls, a stove, a crooked table and boxes of food. The stove was throwing off waves of heat. Hi threw his gear against the back wall. Fenk was unloading Big Nose and Crabby, putting them in the corral with the others. Wacky, who had stayed at the camp all week, had fresh coffee perking, antelope steaks frying and a pot of boiled potatoes. They ate outside where Fenk built a campfire and hit the hay before it was full dark.

"First light," said Fenk softly, shaking him. Wacky was already at the stove cooking bacon and stirring the sourdough batter. They drank the coffeepot dry, saddled up and rode out. The hundred-mile sight line eased Hi's mind away from money worries.

The sun was up by the time they got to the spring. There were plenty of fresh horse tracks and piles of dung.

"They come for water after dark," said Fenk in his woman's voice, "with their tongues hanging out for a drink. You follow me? They don't never come in the daylight."

It took the three of them all day to dig four-foot holes and set the posts—old sawed-off telephone poles—and string the cable and wire. Wacky and Fenk built the wings while Hi hauled juniper and sagebrush to disguise them.

It was late afternoon, about three hours before dark, the sky filling with braided clouds evasive in direction, when they finished. They went back to camp to pack up. Fenk whispered they would go home because it was going to rain and he didn't want to get the car stuck, let the horses have a week or two to get used to the change in the landscape, then they would come out, take their places before dusk and wait until night fell and the horses came to drink, then jump up and close the trap. They'd leave the horses there to fill up on water. They would be easier to handle the next morning that way when they'd be roping and hobbling them and driving them to the rail yard at Wamsutter, thirty miles distant.

"Then where do they go?" asked Hi. He guessed they would be rodeo stock.

Fenk sniggered. "Mink farms. California pet food factories. Chicken feed. Follow me?"

Ten days later they caught seventeen horses. Fenk said it was a good trap, no telling how long they could use it; months, maybe. The hardest work was getting them to the railroad and into the hot, airless car. Those cars smelled like death, and Hi felt his stomach roil. Horses kept coming to the trap and in between days they searched for additional springs and flowing wells.

Fenk had a dozen tricks to slow chicken horses down on the drive to the railroad. He would catch a horse, make a slit in a nostril, run a length of rawhide through and tie it closed, reducing the animal's oxygen intake. Or he would tie two horses together, or tie one to a broke saddle horse. A few got a big metal nut tied into their forelocks, the constant hit of the sharp-corner nut causing enough pain to slow them down. The ones who moved too quickly with front hobbles got side hobbles. And obstreperous horses that continued to fight to get free despite everything he gutshot.

"What the hell, Fenk!" cried Hi the first time his brother-in-law put up his rifle and shot a breakaway stallion. For two days the animal listlessly plodded after the other horses. It was still standing when they reached the tracks.

"They stay alive long enough," murmured Fenk matter-of-factly. "Hey, they're headed for chicken feed anyway, you follow me? What difference does it make? Still worth five or six bucks."

But Hi thought it was an ugly business and when the day came that Fenk told him to shoot two of the fighters he quit. He said it as it came to him, without reflection.

"Well, you'll walk then. Go ahead. I'm not fixin to throw a fit over you." Fenk's eyebrows pulled together in a black, hairy stripe. His whispering voice rasped like a file. "You wasn't with us from the git-go, am I right? You're so lily-livered you can have a good long hike to think it over."

"I thought it over." Hi walked three miles to the tent camp, got his bedroll and necessaries and hiked through the night to the old stage road where, in early morning light, he caught a ride with Isidore the Jew peddler, riding in the back of his wagon and watching a handful of magpies chop the air into black and white flashes.

Helen put Mercurochrome on his blisters and bandaged his raw feet.

"I can't understand why you quit that way," she said. "What are we goin to do now?"

"Get out a this hellhole. Far as Fenk's concerned I'm sage-brushed for good. Wasn't makin enough to do much for the bank anyways. You might as well know they are takin the place. Move up to Rock Springs or Superior. We'll rent. I'll get a job in the coal mines. That's steady money and I won't have to shoot anybody in the guts." He told her about Fenk's ways with wild horses.

"The poor things," she said, for Helen had a tender heart. "I guess Fenk has got a mean streak."

"It's the money, I suppose. He's one will do anything to get it. You ought to see how he's wrecked the new car. Figures he can get another one easy."

"Maybe he can," said Helen. Fenk seemed to her now a cruel monster. She vowed never to speak to him again.

They were not hiring at Superior but he found work at the Union Pacific mines in Rock Springs. Even though the company house was more of a shack Helen liked the conveniences of town—electricity, running water. The kids could walk to school. There were plenty of people around, gossip and talk, a social life, handy food supplies. That pleasure sagged when little Riffie got

113

sick with polio and had to be put in an iron lung. The doctor told Helen that it was living in town and going to school with other children that had caused it, that polio was contagious, and that in their old homestead out on the edge of the desert the child would likely have remained free of the affliction. Helen hated the doctor, not the town.

1940

The coal mines were hard for a man who'd once owned his place and worked all his life outdoors. Hi was surprised to find he missed horse catching with Fenk, riding through the chill high desert, the grey-green sage and greasewood, the salt sage sheltering sage hens, pronghorn, occasional elk, riding up on ridges and mesas to spy out bands of wild horses, plodding through the sand dunes, seeing burrowing owls in a prairie dog town, wheeling ferruginous hawks and eagles, a solitary magpie flying across the quilted sky like a driven needle, the occasional rattlesnake ribboning away. Seeking the elusive water flows and seeps had given him a private, solitary pleasure that he could not share with anyone. Not even Helen could understand the pull of the wild desert. And as much as he despised Fenk's ways, the man loved the wild country and it was a bond. Now, to go down in a metal cage with men in stinking garments unchanged for weeks or months, to work bent over in a cramped space in dim light was misery. He dragged home late, black with coal dust. Helen had a tub of hot water ready for him at night, a very great luxury. Because of the new war in Europe—they were calling it World War Two, demoting the Great War to World War One—the work held steady, he spoke less, went daily to the job as an automaton. Two years cranked by.

Helen mourned the separation from her sister but could not stomach the thought of Fenk. The children whined and belly-ached to see their cousins again. Verla wrote to her pleading, explaining and describing a Fenk Helen did not know, a sensitive "deep" Fenk. It took time, but at last Verla wore Helen down and Helen gave in, persuaded Hi they had to make amends for the sake of the children and Verla. Thanksgiving was named as the day for reconciliation and rejoicing.

Verla and Fenk and their four children drove into town Thanks-giving morning in their 1939 Crosley, even Fenk, who was rough but bragged that he did not hold a grudge, keyed up. Verla bal-anced a packed basket on her knees and the girls clutched boxes of cake and jams. Immediately the country and town cousins ran down to the railroad tracks to throw stones at the bums in the hobo jungle and at the great huffing engines. The shining steel rails, surely the most polished objects on earth, awed the Fipps cousins.

"You got a penny?" asked Buster. The cousins shook their backcountry heads.

"Too bad. You put a penny on the rail, see, and the train comes and mashes it flat and big and skinny."

"Yeah," said Henry. "And that ain't all. This kid in our school, Warren McGee, got his legs cut off. He was runnin on the ties and the train was comin and his sister yelled at him to get off but he tripped and the train got him."

"Did he die?"

"Naw. He goes to school at home. The teacher comes to his house. He's got this wheelchair and his sister pushes him around."

"Did he say it hurt?"

"What a you think? Course it hurt."

The house was redolent of pies and simmering giblet gravy.

Helen had raised two turkeys in the minuscule backyard, had slaughtered and plucked them two days earlier. She put them in the oven at seven, aiming at midafternoon. Verla brought side dishes and relishes—pickled black walnuts, red pepper relish, vinegar pie and a dish of Hattie Bailey, which she and Helen remembered from Thanksgiving at their paternal grandmother's house.

"Where did you get okra!" marveled Helen. Verla smirked and finally admitted a distant cousin had sent it in the mail and the pods had arrived in usable condition. The girls and women worked in the kitchen, punching down the dough for the rolls, grating carrots and cabbage for slaw, making celery curls and radish roses, arranging olives on a saucer with their red eyes glaring outward, all talking a mile a minute to catch up. Hi and Fenk talked politics at first, both hating FDR who had dragged them into this Hitler war. Fenk bragged about his Crosley which he claimed got better than fifty miles to the gallon. Hi said the coal mining business was changing.

"They're puttin in these machines for what they call 'strip mining,' put us old boys out a business."

"Well," said Fenk, "oil is the direction to look, I think. Fella I know got in it two years ago and today he is sittin pretty."

"You still catchin horses?" asked Hi.

"Yeah. Well, not so much like we used to. I throwed in with Tolbert for a while after Wacky went up to Montana. So now I pretty much run em. Lot a fun, don't hurt them none. You got a dodge the oil geologists. Desert is crawlin with those bastards. You ought a come out with us, get out a that hole in the ground for a while. You used a be able to throw a loop. Do you good."

Hi said it would sure enough do him good. He hated the underground. He said he would, and before the women called dinner he had agreed to ride out the next weekend with Fenk.

"If it ain't snowin a blizzard. Could start any day now."

"We had that little swipe in September."

"I got a real good horse you can ride. Little buckskin, come out a the Chain Lakes two years ago. Throws his head up real snooty like, so we call him 'Senator Warren.'"

Hi laughed.

The chase was exhilarating. He had missed the keen wind, the badlands and outlaw cliffs, the smell of horses, the distant prong-horn sentry alert and wound up, the whinnying dust cloud. Fenk flung his arm out. They went after the band, cutting northeast at a sharp angle to head them off, but keeping two miles behind the rises to avoid showing themselves. They rode with Tolbert's two oldest boys, Hi on Senator Warren, his old rope coiled and ready. Fenk had built a trap in the heart of the badlands of casually interwoven sage and rabbitbrush to guide a herd into a box canyon with steep-sloped stone walls. But even as Hi rejoiced in the broken country, he could see changes had come in the two years he'd been digging coal. There were fences where no fences had ever been, and the old White Moon trail had become a county road, complete with culverts and ditches. There were wisps of wool in the sage and greasewood so he supposed the sheepmen had been using the desert for wintering their woolies.

Once inside the trap Fenk and the Tolberts leaped from their mounts and ran to close the opening with three heavy cables. They could hear the horses at the end of the trap coming up point-blank against the stone walls. The old stallion was scream-ing with rage, and even from the mouth of the trap they could see the powdery dust cloud that rose from frantic horses trying to scale unscalable walls. And yet somehow, almost beyond belief, one horse clawed its way up and began to run west.

Hi, outside the gate, was the only one mounted. Automatically he took up the chase, Senator Warren understanding the game well. The escaped horse, a young bay, was hurt and exhausted. Climbing that thirty-foot almost sheer wall had taken a lot of the starch out of him. Hi built a loop and within a mile of the trap roped the escaped prisoner. But the terrified and furious horse drew on inner reserves of strength and fairly dragged Senator Warren with him. One of the new fence corners loomed. The wild horse dodged around it sharply. The sudden swerve broke the old rope. The bay staggered a step or two, then ran. Hi's end of the rope leaped back and wrapped around Senator Warren's ankles. The Senator began to buck, the rope tangling and twisting. Hi saw the fence coming closer and rather than get piled into it, he bailed out of the saddle, hit the ground and rolled. As he rolled one of Senator Warren's lashing hind feet clipped him on the thigh.

In a minute one of the Tolbert boys was there, catching up the Senator's reins. Fenk and the other Tolbert boy galloped up.

"Hell, I'm all right," said Hi. "Everthing's fine. Just my leg's a little bit busted. I guess I can get some time off from work now." He laughed, and Fenk laughed with him, relieved that he wasn't bad hurt. The Tolbert boys sat dazed, dusty and wordless.

"Okay, just lay there," said Fenk. "I'm goin a get the Crosley and we'll get you into town, get that leg set."

"Not much I can do except lay here," said Hi. "I promise I won't run off."

Fenk went to get his automobile, and the Tolbert boys got down and squatted near Hi. They smoked cigarettes, lighting one for Hi. The oldest boy pulled out a half-empty pint of whiskey and offered it; Hi took a good slug.

"That was a good catch. Reckon your rope was old?"

"Hell, yes. Couple years I didn't use it. They say ever year you don't use a rope it loses half its strength. How about that old horse climb up that wall?"

Fenk was back with the Crosley after a wide hour and they loaded Hi into the backseat. There was no room for the Tolbert boys who rode back to the horse trap. Business was business.

All the way to Rock Springs Hi joked and laughed, said he had had a fine day, that he'd just as soon quit the coal mine before the strip machinery came in and go back to chasing horses with Fenk.

"Stop at the house first," he said. "I'll let Helen know I'm okay. Otherwise she'll be up at the hospital devilin everybody."

Helen came out on the porch as Fenk pulled up. She had the fearful-woman look on her face. She leaned in, staring at Fenk, not seeing Hi in the back.

"What's wrong!" She knew it was bad if Fenk was alone. Her old dislike of her sister's husband, who caused harm to all around him, rose, flared anew.

From the backseat Hi called out that he was fine, and she cried a little, saying they really had her going there for a minute.

"They'll set the leg at the hospital and Fenk can bring me home. What's for dinner?" He laughed.

At the emergency entrance of the hospital Fenk parked near the door and walked in. It took him ten minutes to find anyone. He came back with Doc Plumworth whose mouth was so small only two teeth showed when he smiled, the cross-eyed nurse and a gurney. Doc opened the back door of the Crosley and pulled at Hi's arm.

"It's okay, fella, we'll get you fixed up," he said in his crackery voice. He pulled again, turned to Fenk. "Thought you said he was in good spirits. Thought you said he was conscious."

"Christ, he is. Horse kicked him in the leg, that's all. I been kicked a hunderd times myself. Talked and laughed all the way in. Told jokes. Just stopped by his house to see his wife couple minutes ago."

Doc Plumworth, half in the backseat, had been examining Hi.

"Well, he's not telling jokes now. He's dead. Horse kicked him? I'll bet you . . ."

Helen heard Fenk's Crosley outside again. That was pretty quick, she thought. The coffee was perking and she was reheating the lamb stew. She opened the door to Fenk. He stood there, working his mouth, glutinously whispered something like "clot," then looked at her with his great staring eyes. Her mind snarled like a box of discarded fiddle strings. Civilization fell away and the primordial communication of tensed muscle, ragged breath, the heaving gullet and bent fingers spoke where language failed. She knew only what Fenk had not yet said and didn't need to say.

And shut the door in his face.

Deep-Blood-Greasy-Bowl

During construction of our house the builders unearthed an ancient fire pit. Carbon 14 testing indicated an age of 2,500 years, centuries before the Indians had horses or bows and arrows. Other fire pits, nearby tipi rings, projectile points and a chert quarry attest to long Indian presence on the land. Facing the house is a limestone cliff where a bison drive over the edge may have occurred in ancient days. Imagining the time and the hunt made this small story.

Gradually the familiar sounds of night and sleep gave way. A few men came awake at once and raised up on their elbows, listening to the change. The chill air presaged autumn. In the blue draw coyotes argued. A sated owl on the island hooted and the river choked through sunbaked stones. But these were common sounds, and had not wakened the men. Silence disturbed their sleep, the cessation of a voice. The shaman had stopped chanting. Night after night the thready monotone of his prayers and invocations had formed the solemn background of the band's dreaming. His beckoning, coaxing voice had become as elemental as chirring grasshopper wings or the rattle-stick cries of flying cranes. Forbidden to eat during the ceremonial invocation the old man had grown gaunt and his voice had wavered almost to inaudibility. But now he was quiet, task completed, and into the vacuum of silence rushed excitement.

The men who had immediately wakened—the hunters—strained for the aural vanishing point, those sounds too remote for all but the inner ear. The need to put on fat, to store food against the hungry winter slinking toward them made them exquisitely sensitive to nuances of the natural world: strong clouds rubbing against the sky like a finger drawn over skin, the quiver of a single blade of grass in calm air showing subterranean movement. Some could tell by the briny smell of seaweed when storms were advancing from the distant ocean. A few branches of cottonwood leaves had already turned an urgent yellow; the first frosts hung over them like veils of thin rain not yet touching the ground.

Below their suspirations and heartbeats, they sensed the roaring of bison deep inside the earth, a bellowing that made bedrock quiver and promised that something long-awaited was about to happen. The shaman's silence allowed the promise to become a hot expectation of blood and meat, for bison, in their wandering journey through the world, were surely moving toward them.

The men rose and went outside to relieve themselves in the sagebrush, stared at the sky for its message. It was flat and colorless in the predawn as though rubbed by an antler polishing tool. It said nothing. It would be a hot, breathless day, affirming that summer still lay on them like a panting wolf on a red bone.

The hunters asked each other, How many? It was crucial to know how many.

It had been years since a herd had come within driving distance of the cliff, but because it had happened in the past at the end of one summer the band had continued to camp near the foot of the precipice, knowing it would happen again. The river lay between their camp and the pale limestone cliff. It was summer's end and the hard sun had incinerated all rain clouds until the river barely skimmed the gravel bars. At the base of the cliffs a strip of brushy ground fronted steep talus slopes, the millennial accumulation of debris from crumbling rock. The last time the driven animals had plunged into the terrifyingly steep chimney, some finally rolling down the talus slope, others piling up on it, a mass of kick-leg flesh. The butcher women had rushed at them with their biface chert knives, skinning and slicing tools, pitched the offal into the gulping river.

From the tipi camp on the south side of the river every detail of the cliff face and the lives of the animals and birds who lived in and on it dominated their view. A small band of mountain sheep moved around the upper benches out of range, sometimes gazing haughtily down at them, sometimes still and bunched like pale fists. A pair of eagles and their two grown young played in the updrafts above the cliff, their thin, tumbling calls requests for prayers. As always, the young men made plans to capture them for their feathers, but they also begged the eagles to carry their wishes for a successful hunt to the spirits. There was a thrilling moment that sent chills down their spines when the eagles separated in the air and flew to the four sacred directions. Never had there been such a strong sign of the future.

In the spring one of the hunters, now a mature man but only a boy the last time the bison had allowed themselves to be driven over this cliff, had dreamed that this year they would come again. They would come through the east pass. They were coming, he knew it, a black mass pouring out of their deep hole into sunlight, stirring the powdery earth into dust clouds. He dreamed of spurting bright blood, slippery and strength-giving, coursing down the chins of his children, the yielding juiciness of fresh liver warm from a beast that moments before had been running out its life. He woke from the dream with the taste of liver and spicy gall in his mouth. The shaman also remembered that earlier hunt and said the man's dream was a true dream.

The intensity of the hunter's memory of the kill many seasons earlier had commanded attention from the others. Their tipi skins were old and patched, and so, in early summer they made the journey to that jump-off place. There were other reasons than bison to come here; innumerable sego lilies grew in a certain draw where in spring the women dug the bulbs with antler points; goosefoot and biscuit-root grew nearby. There was rice-grass around the sand dunes, fish, beaver and mink in the river, pronghorn and deer feeding along the waterway and the moun-tain sheep on the cliff. Countless birds and thousands of small animals lived in this rich riparian habitat.

On the great downslope atop the cliff the men and boys strengthened the old drive lines of stones with additional rocks, white lumps of limestone that showed even in twilight. Beside the western cairn marking the edge, the hunters dug a hiding pit for the shaman, who would pull the bison forward by incantation and the luring sound of his flute. When they finished, the heaps of stones extended out in lines from the top of the cliff toward the distant pass. The bison would come from that direction. It was the only possible direction. Near the top of the cliff a brushy draw, the upper end of the sego lily slope, angled toward the point where the drive line hooked inward to compress the herd. As the animals moved up the grade toward the drop-off, the flanking drivers would rise from hollows in the ground, from concealing sagebrush, and press them into panic. If the herd began to veer toward the shelter of the draw, the boys and young men concealed in that earth crease would rise up ululating and turn them irrevocably toward the edge. It was dangerous and beautiful, this death run with the bison. That was how it had been done in the earlier time. That was how they would do it again. It was what they had been born for.

Some men went to the chert vein that erupted along a ridge beyond the sand dunes, worrying the desirable nodules coated with white calcareous cortex from the earth. They would carry as many as they could back to the camp, bury them in the earth and build a fire on top for the slow heat treatment that made chert glossy and easy to work. Later, from the tempered chert they could strike good cores for making scrapers, projectiles and knife blades.

The hunter who had been a boy at the time of the previous hunt spoke again, as he had many times, of the sand dunes near the base of the great slope where the drivers had to work with the wind, not letting themselves be seen but guiding the keen-nostriled beasts between the drive lines by the presence of alien human odor. The others had heard all this and seen the terrain each fruitless year when no bison came or only a too-small group that could not be driven. The hunter once more told them how the stampeders lying hidden behind sagebrush, badger tumuli and prairie dog mounds leapt up from the earth at the vital moment and confronted the bison. The terrified animals lost their reason, became mad creatures who rushed blindly forward, kicking up rocks and clods of threadleaf sedge with dark roots like tangled drowned man's hair, trampling snakes and grasshoppers, some stumbling, and the others rushing over animals trying vainly to rise. They were no longer bison but meat. That was how it had happened years before.

Again the hunters asked each other, How many? It was crucial to know how many.

Two young men said they would go and find the herd, determine its size, direction of travel and speed. A young boy of ten summers pleaded to come with them. When an infant his ears had frozen and the stubbed remnants gave him an animal appearance; he was Small Marmot. They headed east toward the mountain north of the pass at a distance-eating half trot. Was the herd large enough to be stampeded? Small groups did not succumb to mass hysteria. And the tipi skins were old.

It was late in the day when the young men returned. They had circled around, returning from the north where the precipice was low, allowing easy descent to the river ford and the camp on the far side. While still on high ground they stood looking at the camp below pressed by the stunning weight of light that hammered the earth's thin rind. The light seemed to pull at the tipis, pulling them loose to rise into twittering molecules of sky. The flood of brilliance offered a merciless clarity of view. In a few weeks autumn wildfire smoke would blur and erase the mountains, the wind would thicken with ash and dust, but now the still air was like pure water and all appeared as distinct as pebbles at the bottom of a spring. They heard a thin sound, rising and quivering like the kestrel hovering over prey. The old shaman had eaten and slept, regaining enough strength to play his flute, the sound that was even then ineluctably pulling the bison to them.

The stub-eared boy gazing down into the camp could see the fringe of shining hairs outlining a puppy's ears. As he stared the shaman's tipi seemed to tremble, losing its solid outline, becoming as transparent as new ice so that he could see everything inside. He could see the band's sacred treasure, a deep stone bowl that had come to them in the distant past. It was a soft and gleaming grey color veined with pale and dark streaks, and men said that to the touch it felt greasy. After a successful bison hunt it was rubbed with fat which further darkened the stone. Power emanated from the bowl. It craved blood. It needed fat. It was very heavy; two men were necessary to lift it even when it was empty. Because it was a spiritual treasure and because it had power, when they traveled they wrapped it in white deer hides with spiritual herbs, and it was drawn by dog travois. Small Marmot could feel its grey force pulling the bison closer, the bowl thirsty for the blood that would brim to its cold lip.

The young men and the boy told the hunters the bison were moving slowly toward the slope. It was a good herd. The three of them extended their fingers six times to show how many. The flute was drawing the animals. They could not help themselves. They were coming. They would be on the slope in the morning.

Now time began to mass together in the shape and color of bison. Nothing else had importance. The women examined their tipi skins, calculating how many new ones were needed. The waiting men struck long, slender cores from the cooled chert. Someone brought out a fine piece of obsidian from the northwest, the shining black stone responding to his touch as a child to his father. They finished and repaired thrusting spears, chipped fresh edges on skinning tools and knives. The young men, keyed up with excitement to the point of agony, wanted to get in place along the drive line before darkness fell. The hunters told them there would be time in the morning, that the bison would not arrive at the bottom of the great slope before the sun was high. Patience was essential in a hunt of this kind. Still, many lay awake all night, burning for the morning. Before they went on top of the cliff, the hunters, preceded by the shaman, carried the Deep-Blood-Greasy-Bowl to the butchering site where the bison would fall. They set it carefully on a large flat rock marked by an eagle feather.

As they came up over the cliff they could see the herd near the bottom of the slope. The evening before the bison had gone to the river and taken on huge quantities of water and were now recovering from the lethargy induced by deep drinking. The wind was out of the northwest. The shaman went to the declivity near the western cairn and began to call the herd on his flute. The men and boys took their places along the drive lines, in the sand dunes, behind burrowing animals' rubble heaps, in the sego lily draw. The sun stumped along the hot sky and the bison drifted slowly up the slope. They passed the sand dunes where the scent of the hunters hidden there carried to them indirectly and faintly, just enough to make some of them slightly uneasy. Several bulls threw up their heads as though to get a stronger sense of it, but the herd kept grazing uphill.

When the sand dunes were behind them and they were a critical distance from the edge of the precipice, the men and boys at the rear of the drive lines stood up, shouting, flapping deerskins and running at the bisons' flanks. The startled herd veered west and twenty yelling men rose up. The animals at the front began to run, and when one ran, all ran. The herd coalesced, bunching up as the yelling boys and men flanked, moving faster until they were galloping upslope with staring but unseeing eyes, bumping each other, metamorphosing into a vast living animal with hundreds of legs.

Near the top the final group of hunters hidden in the west-hooking draw sprang up and forced the bison to pack together even more tightly in a galloping, insane crush from which it was impossible to escape. One of the young men dashed too close and was sucked into the hoofed landslide. The first animals went over the edge roaring and breaking off chunks of limestone, falling, flailing, flying, their legs still running as they tumbled through the air. Rocks fell with the bison in an earthquake of impact. Smothering clouds of dust rose. From below the hunters heard the shrieks and fierce cries of the women amid the dying bellows of broken bison. The last of the herd went over and the hunters dared to approach the edge.

Some animals had fallen on a projecting ledge where they tried to rise on broken legs or with shattered pelvises. Already a few magpies were pulling at open wounds and ravens spiraling down. Most of the bison had fallen or rolled all the way to the talus slope, killed by the impact; some even now were being eviscerated by the women. Men waiting at the bottom with spears and stone axes killed the survivors. None must live, for they would tell the secret of the invisible cliff to other bison.

At the top the hunters discovered the trodden remains of the young man who had gone too close to the running herd, now pulverized into bloody mud. His wife would not rejoice in the massive kill. But that news had not yet reached her and she, with the others, sliced and tore, cut still-pulsing throats and caught the blood in deerskin bags and clay pots. The hunters began scrambling down a precipitous cliff path some distance away, eager for the good rich meat.

The Deep-Blood-Greasy-Bowl stood on the eagle feather rock. To it the women brought their smaller containers of still-smoking blood, and the level in the stone bowl rose steadily higher. The stub-eared boy stood close and stared. Then it was full, so full the convex surface liquid rose slightly above the bowl's containing rim. A paw of wind ribbed the surface. The high blood and the ritual that followed twined into his lifelong sense of existence. The eagles cried sweetly and tenderly over-head, the old pair gliding down to feed on a broken animal on the high ledge. No one doubted that the birds remembered the last drive and would aid them in the next one.

Swamp Mischief

It was a fine summer morning, a day predicted to break all heat records. The Devil sat at his fireproof metal desk enjoying a Havana cigar and a triple espresso while he read *The New York Times, The Guardian* and the Botswana *Survivor* (asbestos editions). He asked Duane Fork, his private secretary demon, to open the windows so he could enjoy the fresh billows of sulfur from the pits and the stunning vista of multithousands of refineries, ship-breaking yards, oil wells and methane gas pads stretching to the horizon. On the wall hung a steel plate depicting the reverse image of Krakatoa exploding. When he had finished the cigar, the coffee and the papers, he checked his e-mail. As usual, no one had sent anything to Devil@hell.org except spammers promising a larger penis, hot stocks, cut-rate office supplies and surefire weight loss.

"Duane!"

"Yessir?" Duane Fork, obsequious and insolent at the same time, half secretary, half butler, was a heavy man with smoldering pants cuffs (when he wore pants) and raccoon eyes who walked as though climbing the steps of a guillotine. Like many shamblers he was a bad speller and so awkward that sometimes, when sitting, he missed the chair.

"Fetch some e-mail," said the Lord of Darkness. Although he

rarely received any messages himself, the Devil had ordered a few of his hackers roasting over eternal fires to collect strangers' e-mail from the Upper World. He had been bored the last few hundred years with very little to do but wait ever since he had put certain observations of steam kettles into the head of a young Scots inventor. The kettle epiphany had booted a species—selfish, clever creatures with poor impulse control, suited to hunt, gather and scratch a little agriculture—into a savagely technological civilization that got rapidly out of hand and sent them blundering toward The End.

"A few hundred years, they'll all be here with me," he murmured. And while he waited for the self-reaping harvest he amused himself by manipulating those humans. He adored fashion, and got to as many designers' openings as he could. He it was who had inspired the butt-freezing Algonquin breechclout, the top-heavy Viking "dilemma" helmet, the intestine-withering whalebone corset and, most recently, transparent nylon gauze trousers for men. He had the warmest feelings for Manolo Blahnik and had ordered a suite prepared for his occupancy with tiger-skin rugs, silver fittings, auk-down comforters and lead crystal decanters. The suite de luxe was equipped with a floor heated to 140 degrees F, and the only shoes waiting in the capacious closet were man-size copies of the master's own designs. If all went well the Devil had him marked for demon training.

One of the Devil's happier pastimes was to read and act upon other's e-mail messages as if they were addressed to him, to spread agreeable waves of havoc and confusion. For their retrieval services the hackers earned a little respite from their personal barbecues, and the Devil enjoyed the sensation of conducting important business.

"Yessir. What category—ordinary correspondence, World Bank messages or government correspondence? And if the latter, which governments?"

The Devil chose the day's category by randomly opening one of his many unabridged dictionaries and, eyes shut, placing his finger on a page. He had pointed up "ornithologist."

"Wonderful! Get me e-mails of ornithologists in Iceland—and America!"

"Including Canada?"

"No Canadian stuff today. I'm in no mood for their so-called civility. Get me stuff from the western states." The Devil had felt himself a westerner ever since he noticed vain cowboys cramming their feet into tiny, high-heeled boots. Here was a fashion that suited the Hoofed One very well, and he had a rare collection of boots decorated with pitchforks, flames licking up from the insteps, an assortment that complemented his numerous bolo ties. (Readers who dispute the Devil's western identity have only to look at the maps—in Montana the Devil's Corkscrew, the Devil's Bedstead in Idaho, in Colorado his favorite Devil's Armchair and in California, of course, the Devil's Kitchen. His bathtub, filled with hot scratchy sand, can be found in Arizona.)

He was, in fact, something of a clotheshorse. After the Fall, the Devil, once the most beautiful of angels, changed beyond recognition. His rosy complexion metamorphosed into leathery grey sharkskin which kaleidoscoped constantly to thick yellow hair, to scales and exaggerated toenails, to heavy red hide or a dull blue dappled with sores. It was his vanity to show himself occasionally to mortal painters, and he was pleased that the walls of the world were hung with art showing him with antlers, with pronged horns, with tusks, with claws, with hair snakes and limp fuzz, with slavering red lips and goats' eyes. In his main closet hung tight silk skins in every color. Drawers of featherless wings, many of them enlarged bat wings in stainless steel and other materials such as vinyl or glue-stiffened burlap, lay folded neatly. In a locked bottom drawer to which only he had the key, covered by a gauze veil, reposed the sole relic of his heavenly past—a pair of exquisite butterfly wings. Two painters, Hieronymus Bosch and Brueghel the Elder, had not seen but dreamed them into paint. Jackson Pollock had also dreamed the Devil's wings, but the painting has been lost.

In the day's batch of e-mails there was little correspondence between Icelandic ornithologists, but a fairly rich harvest from the American west. Most of the messages had to do with an upcoming bird symposium on the theme of the evolution of delayed plumage maturation. His eyes gleamed, for along with fashion shows, rock concerts, amusement parks (he it was who gave Viliumas Malinauskas the idea for Stalin World), he delighted in symposia. He made a note of the date in his calendar.

A message from a biologist at a national park, someone who signed himself Argos, caught his eye. The Devil recalled Argos— Odysseus's dog, the only one who remembered his master after his grinding travels. He knew what most human historians did not—that Argos, who had never liked Odysseus, did not greet him with smiles and wagging tail, but lifted his black lip and growled.

The ornithologist Argos wrote to someone named James Tolbert:

Jim buddy, how goes it? Lousy here. Times I want to put Burton through the pencil sharpener. Another damn management meeting that went on for three hours. They all treat me like I'm the janitor. Burton bows and flatters the wolf biologist, the mountain lion biologist, the bear man. Me? I'm just the bird guy, no power, no clout. The ones that count are the guys who deal with big animals that can kill people. What I need is a big dangerous bird. I'd sell my soul for a pterodactyl. They'd pay attention then you bet, especially after a couple tourists got carried off.

*　　*　　*

"Carpe diem!" said the Devil. "Duane!"

"Yessir?"

"What do you know about pterodactyls?" He pronounced the "p" very distinctly.

"I believe the pterodactyl was some kind of flying dinosaur, sir. I think it lived in the Jurassic."

"You bet. Great times, the Jurassic. Dig out some background. Didn't we get the pterodactyl started on feathers?"

"I don't know, sir. That was before my time."

A heavy envelope was sent up from Hell's research department and the Devil shuffled through the stack of photographs of skeletons and reconstructions.

"That one looks like my cousin." He glanced briefly at his own reflection in his mirrored ashtray. "Well, let's see. Maybe I'll give this Argos a few sets of pterodactyls. Say about four to start. Go get one of those women who used to make the science films for the BBC so we can find out what pterodactyls eat. We might have to rearrange some of the habitat in Argos's park."

The television woman, Malvina Sprout, came in at a half run. She smelled of charred hair and her hands and arms were black with soot.

"Sir?"

"You know what pterodactyls eat?"

"Pterodactyls? Is this a test? Do I get time off from the flamethrower if I get it right?"

The Devil frowned fearfully and the woman shrank back.

"I'm not sure. Ferns, maybe? Cycads? I think cycads?"

"Don't they eat meat?"

"I'm not sure. It's been a long time and I don't have any of my source material here. We never did much with pterodactyls."

"Okay. Back to your flamethrower, sister." He drummed his fingers, adjusted his chain-link tie. "Duane!"

"Yessir?"

"See if we've got some dinosaur people here. Get me an expert. And check the bestiary, see if we've got any pterodactyls on hand." He sucked at the end of his tail for a little pick-me-up. (The iconography of Hell often shows the Devil with a harpoon blade at the end of his caudal extremity, an error promulgated by ecclesiastical historians of yesteryear. In fact, the terminal of the Devil's tail is fitted with a carved ivory stopper, for the tail, like Toulouse-Lautrec's walking stick, is hollow, allowing the introduction of various liquids and sauces. The Devil keeps his tail charged with fine Spanish brandy.)

The summoned expert, Professor Bracelet Quean, was not the most reliable authority as he had earned his place in the Devil's simmering tar pit through plagiarism and fakery; he knew little about pterosaurs or any other extinct creature. But old rhetorical habits never die and he puffed and swaggered as though in possession of the most intimate knowledge.

"What did they eat? Well, let's just see now." He paused for effect. "I would say fish, they ate fish." There was another pause.

"Snakes." He was silent for nearly a minute. "And ducks and birds. Insects—the giant dragonflies of the Jurassic, you know—and probably some plants. Cycads."

"Cycads, eh?"

"Yes. Cycads are rather like giant carrots."

"Make a note, Duane."

Duane wrote down "cicads."

"And what sort of habitat?"

"Swamps. Heavy, moist, extensive swamps. And shallow seas. Very warm and moist climate." The professor was cooking now. "They'd skim over the seas snapping up ducks and flying fish. There would have been plenty of palm trees and giant horsetails. And the giant carrots."

The Devil looked glum. It was one thing to throw together a few cacti and some scorpions, but an inland sea and extensive swamps called for advanced engineering and almost certainly a rearrangement of the yearly budget. Still, he had all those interstate highway engineers—he could put them to work. Perhaps they could skip the inland sea and make do with just the swamp. And if worse came to worst he would go to Plan B although it strained his powers.

"*El visible universo era una ilusión,*" he said, quoting Borges. "Okay. Back to the book mutilation section, Professor. And snap it up!" His index finger released a stinging green ray that caught the academic on his left buttock.

The first to notice anything unusual was a retired hog farmer from Missouri. On his way out of the park he saw a ranger scraping canine ordure from the sole of his high-laced boot and stopped to talk.

"You know, I thought I was in Missoura there for a while—all them cicadas—just like in the Mark Twain National Forest back home. I didn't think you-all had cicadas out here."

"We don't. Where did you see them?"

"Didn't *see* them. Heard them. Thousands and thousands. Up in that swamp. They don't live in swamps back home."

"Swamp?"

"Yep. Show you on the map." He pointed at the north corner where two lakes—Big Gramophone and Little Gramophone— were joined by a small stream.

"Thought I'd try a little fishing at the lakes here, and I hiked in, but there's no lakes, just a swamp. I seen a cowboy in there and asked him but he just took off. Guess you been in a bad drought situation?"

"It has been a little dry," said the ranger, thinking that the lakes had looked high and full only two weeks earlier. Maybe the man had missed the trail. He tried to remember any swampy areas near the lakes.

"Well, I say you got some mighty powerful cicadas. Hope you get some rain and get those lakes filled up. It's probably globular warming. So long."

"Vaya con Dios," said the ranger, thinking he might take a run up to the Gramophones.

In Hell there was a commotion. There were no pterodactyls; a selection of English sparrows, the omnipresent birds of Hell, had had to be biologically modified and enlarged. Then these faux pterodactyls had to be recalled when someone discovered they lacked serious dentition.

"Call these things pterodactyls?" raged the Devil, who cherished the image of shark-mouthed flying horrors in a Frank Frazetta painting. "They look more like pelicans. Get some teeth in these things."

The bestiary manager, who had run a petting zoo in the Upper World, said he thought this was the natural state of the creatures.

"They didn't really have much in the way of teeth, sir."

"I don't care. We'll have our dentists do some implants. I want to see *teeth* before we send them out on their mission. The ornithologist Argos seems to think they had stupendous teeth. Fix them up."

Most of the dentists had earned their way to the nether regions through multiple affairs with receptionists, assistants, hygienists and X-ray techs. Dr. Mavis Brooms had indulged in all of these venereal delights, with the UPS man thrown in for dessert. Still, she had been an excellent dentist and relished the chance to fit a few pterodactyls with teeth. She longed to take photographs of the procedure, write it up and send it to *Experimental Dentistry,* an impossible wish as the only mail that came to Hell consisted of bills for the inhabitants and no mail at all went out. There were computers, but they were programmed to crash randomly five times a minute.

She spent considerable time working out a plan. Because there was no dental lab in Hell she had to persuade a farrier to hammer out the implants. The farrier was a cretin from Bessarabia who had died in 1842 from alcohol poisoning. It was difficult to make him understand what she needed. Anything beyond horseshoes seemed too much for him. In the end he whanged out something passable and Dr. Brooms put an automotive technician to work refining the shapes. The teeth were slightly more successful, fossil shark teeth stolen from a collection at a natural history museum in Valparaiso.

The pterodactyls were difficult patients and had to be strapped into the chair. They fought terribly and, as there was no anesthetic in Hell, moaned, but Dr. Brooms was hardened to moans, which rose from every corner and alley. The results were not good. The pterodactyls could not manage their shark teeth and constantly bit their own lips. Twigs and leaves stuck in the dental interstices. The Devil commanded that the creatures be whetted up on meat and took away their vegetation.

"Give them twenty-four hours' prey-capture training and get them up into that park!" shouted the Devil, "while they can still chew."

*　　*　　*

Park Superintendent Amelia McPherson, seven biologists (including Argos the ornithologist), the ranger and an unknown fellow with a deep sunburn in cowboy boots and bolo tie, presumably someone from Public Relations, gathered at the edge of the swamp. The din of cicadas was extraordinary.

"What about these cicadas?" shouted Fong Saucer, the wolf biologist, a big hirsute man with a nose like a kumquat and an electric yellow beard. "What are they doing here?"

"They must have been introduced," said the ornithologist with a poisonous glance, "like your wolves."

"This horrid swamp," mourned Superintendent McPherson. "Where are my lakes?" For a just-completed aerial survey had showed an extensive swamp but no lakes.

"What is *that*?" said the wolf man, catching sight of a pterodactyl with a thirty-foot wingspread, striking in crimson and green feathers, the primaries edged in black, the breast showing violet spots, gliding toward them through the dead trees.

"*Hilfe!*" shrieked Warwick the bear biologist (raised in Germany, where his father had been stationed) as the pterodactyl bore down on him. It snapped ghastly teeth and released a stream of pterodactyl manure from an oversize cloaca. It wheeled and came back again, its great claws curling for the grab. In seconds the bear biologist was skimming over the swamp. The cicada din was terrific.

"Help me, Gott! Gott, *hilfe,* help!" bellowed the bear man and the pterodactyl dropped him like an oversize hot potato. The biologist fell headfirst into the swamp, sending up a gout of mud and gnawed sticks.

The creature sailed off into the dead snags at the far end of the swamp and they all heard the distant crack of branches as though something heavy had settled in dry limbs. The PR man moved back a little from the group. The shimmering horizon seemed to tilt slightly, as though the phantom cube of spatial balance in each viewer's mind had slipped a little.

"I think we just saw a pterodactyl," said Argos calmly, feeling a tiny but odd grip inside his chest as though someone had nipped a paper clip onto a vague and minor part of his interior works. Then he shrieked, "Just saw a *pterodactyl*! This is better than the ivory-billed woodpecker!" He began to caper and shake his arms. He rolled his head and hissed through his teeth, all the motions and cries one produces when confronted with fabulous impossibilities. A flash of scientific doubt shut him up.

"Got to get Reggie out," said Superintendent Amelia, staring at the kicking legs of the bear biologist. She looked at the swamp. The black water was interrupted by great tussocks of saw-edged grass. Below lay sunken logs slippery with green algae. In the distance something plunged. She reached for her cell phone.

"Hello, Security? I'm out at the swamp—where the lakes used to be. I said, out at the swamp. The noise? It's cicadas. . . . Cicadas! Never mind that. Get a rescue helicopter out here. We've got a man drowning in a mud hole and can't get to him."

But the bear biologist was far from drowning. His head and upper torso were wedged in the remnants of a beaver dam, and while it was not a pleasure retreat, the flow of water was minimal.

"It's the Final Days," he whimpered. He prayed in German and English, for he was a religious man, a member of a group of hallucinated enthusiasts, Penecostal Grizzly Scientists, who met once a month in the back room of a taxidermist's shop. Now he drew heavily on his spiritual bank account, and it seemed to him that with every prayer he uttered the beaver dam structure gave way. In ten minutes he was able to pull himself out of the enmeshed branches. The swamp around him had cleared in a two-meter circle and a path of sparkling water stretched to the shore. He was gripping a log unusually large for a beaver dam, large enough, in fact, to be used as a watercraft.

"It's a miracle," he said. "Thank you, god." Babbling prayers, he began to kick his way to land.

On that shore Argos was peering into the distance hoping to see the pterodactyl return. He wished badly he had brought a camera. He had to record what he was seeing. He owed it to science. He vowed to upgrade to a cell phone with a camera as soon as possible. With anxious hands he searched his pockets, found his folded paycheck and a ballpoint pen that skipped, began to sketch a clumsy impression of what he had seen. Or thought he had seen.

The superintendent was on the phone again.

"Security, cancel that helicopter. Our man is extricating himself. Here they come again!" The PR man took a few steps back.

All four pterodactyls, flying in formation, came quickly from the far end of the dissolving swamp. The park personnel clustered together.

"I don't believe it," said Argos. "This is not happening. This can't happen."

"*Liebe Gott,* our Heavenly Father save us *now,*" muttered the bear biologist squelching along the shore. He could see the others in the distance, the PR man slipping away into the dead trees where, a few moments later, a column of steam indicated a hot spring.

Abruptly everything changed. There was a shower of shark teeth. Four sparrows flew over the lake. The bear man looked at the sky and wept. Argos the ornithologist stared at the paycheck he held in his hand, the outline of a winged lobster scrawled on the back, the paper severely punctured by the point of the bad pen.

"I never believed it," he said. But it was Warwick, the bear biologist, who had grappled with the searing truth when he understood in his marrow that demons were sprinkled throughout the world like croutons in a salad.

Back at his desk, Old Scratch tossed a metal token, a token such as those once used in whorehouses by customers with credit, into a drawer. Inscribed on it was Argos's name and a date.

"Illusions are a real bastard to hold steady," he said. "I'm beat." He tapped idly with his long fingernails for a minute, then took out a pack of cards and began dealing himself poker hands.

"You got to know when to fold them," he said. He shuffled the cards, producing a sound of whirring insect wings.

"The cicadas threw me off," he said.

"Yes sir," answered Duane Fork.

Testimony of the Donkey

Traveler, there is no path. Paths are made by walking.

—Antonio Machado (1875–1939)

M arc was fourteen years older than Catlin, could speak three languages, was something of a self-declared epicure, a rock climber, an expert skier, a not-bad cellist, a man more at home in Europe than the American west, he said, but Catlin thought these differences were inconsequential although she had only been out of the state twice, spoke only American and played no instrument. They met and fell for each other in Idaho, where Marc was working as a volunteer on the fire line and Catlin was dishing up lasagna in the fire center cafeteria. After a few months they began to live together.

He had noticed her muscular legs as she strode along the counter snatching up pans empty of macaroni and cheese and asked her later if she would like to go hiking sometime. For the last two summers Catlin, against her parents' disapproval, had worked on an all-girl hay-stacking crew, and she had hiked Idaho's mountains since she was a child. She was strong and experienced. He knew an excellent trail, he said. She said yes but doubted he could show her any trail she had not hiked.

He picked her up at four on Sunday morning and drove north. By sunrise she had figured it out: "Seven Devils?" He nodded. And he was right. She had never been on the Dice Roll trail. It had a reputation for attracting tourists and she had always imagined it crowded by day-trippers tossing candy wrappers.

As they walked into the fragrant quietude of the pines she was suffused with euphoria, the old mountain trail excitement. Her earliest memory was of trying to clasp pollen-thick sunbeams streaming through stiff needles as she rode in the child carrier on her father's back. She associated the deep green canopy, the rough red bark with well-being. Marc smirked at her; he'd known she would like this trail. They moved in harmony. In midafternoon, her stomach growling with hunger, they reached a spectacular overlook into the chaos of Hell's Canyon. Marc's idea of lunch was two carrots, some string cheese and some fishy paste they scooped out of the container with the carrots. It didn't matter. They had shown each other their lapsarian atavistic tastes, their need for the forest, for the difficult and solitary, for what her father had called "the eternal verities," but which she secretly thought might be ephemeral verities. Yet Catlin's sensibilities tingled with a faint apprehension. She had never expected to meet such a person. Where was the catch?

Their time together stretched into four years. Catlin regaled him with family stories—her sleepwalking grandmother, the alcoholic cousin who fell off a Ferris wheel, her father's steady withdrawal from the family, her mother's generous humor. She told him about her only previous lover, a rapscallion type studying meteorology but now in Iraq. Their affair had been nothing, she said; they had slept together only twice before admitting a growing dislike for each other. Marc was quiet about his past and

Catlin took him on lover's faith. His fine black hair rose in a Mephistophelian aura around his head when the wind blew—it was longer than the locals liked it—and his face bore an arched Iberian nose and narrow eyes with black irises and heavy brows. But in contrast to his darkly handsome face, he was rather short, with thick arms and small hands. He looked a little vicious, like an old artist whose eye is offended by contemporary daubs.

Catlin had been a plump baby with a face like a small pancake. Her adult face was still baby-round with fleshy cheeks and acne scars that gave her a slightly tough streetwise look. The hay-stacking job had made her muscular, an inch taller and ten pounds heavier than Marc. She had man-size feet that had never known high heels. Beauty salon visits lightened and permed her limp blond hair into platinum waves that contrasted with her rough skin. She favored a blue-eyed, parted-lips look popularized by 1930s movie stars. She could hardly know that she resembled his mother.

At the end of the fire season they left Idaho for Lander, Wyoming, where Marc had the promise of a job with an outdoor climbing school. Housing was tight and they finally ended up in a drab single-wide trailer which Catlin said needed more color. She painted the walls cherry red, purple, orange. At a thrift store she found an old round table and sprayed it cobalt blue. A 1960s television set discovered in the shed behind the trailer became one of several shrines to her invented juju gods and fetishes—the Shrine of Never Falling, and the Shrine of Adventure.

"Very oriental," said Marc in a tone that meant nothing. He was thinking of Tibet. After a few months he quit the job at the climbing school, saying only that he couldn't deal with so many flaming egos, didn't like the career life, the business of climbing. Still, he continued to climb with Ed Glide, his only local friend. He switched back to what he had done before firefighting—

freelance work updating information on African countries for travelers' guidebooks, keeping track of insurrections, changing tastes in music and clothing, the whims of dictators. As a child he had lived in Ivory Coast and Zaire, then, as near as Catlin could make out, had spent his adult years in four or five Mediterranean countries. When she asked about that time he talked about plantains in fufu and other dishes. She changed the Shrine of Never Falling to a Shrine of Information for Travelers.

Their landlord was Biff, an elongated, chain-smoking old cowboy with a sweat stain on his hat that resembled the battlements of Jericho. Biff thought he'd discovered the secret of wealth by renting out his dead ex-wife's trailer. He did not like Catlin's color scheme.

"How in hell can I rent this place now? Looks like a carnival." He was so thin he had to buy youth jeans. They were always too short. He stuffed the high-water ends into his run-down work boots.

"Well, you *are* renting it—to us."

"When you're gone," he said, rolling a fresh cigarette with maimed yellow fingers, squinting his triangular eyes against the smoke.

There was nothing to say to that. Only the day before she had asked Marc what he thought about building a cabin. She didn't want to say "house." It sounded too permanent. He only shrugged. That could mean anything. He had that evasive streak and it worried her. She asked once why he had come to Idaho and he answered that he had always wanted to be a cowboy. She had never seen him near a horse or a ranch. Was it a joke?

Catlin had been born and raised in Boise, the great-granddaughter of a Basque shepherd from the Pyrenees, and she sometimes told Marc that that made her European, although she had never been farther away from Idaho than Salt Lake City and Yellowstone Park.

The sheepherder ancestor had been ambitious. He became interested in the criminal physiognomy work of Bertillon and Galton and thought it was possible to make a composite photograph of the Universal Upright Man by overlaying photographs of respected men from every race. The project fell short when he could not find an Inuit, a Papuan, a Bushman or other Idaho rarities to photograph and coalesce. He became cynical about doing good in the world and turned his attention to money, opening a clothing store in Boise, a store that burgeoned into three, enough to provide the family with modest wealth.

Catlin had an allowance from her parents and could have scraped by without working, but she thought it would demoralize Marc. In Wyoming she found a part-time job with the local tourism office and they set her to puzzling out scenic motor tours for massive campers and RVs. That brought about the Shrine of Wide Roads with No Traffic and No Hills.

They maintained the fiction of independence because each owned a vehicle. The real focus of their lives was neither work nor clutching love, but wilderness travel. As many days and weeks as they could manage they spent hiking the Big Horns, the Wind Rivers, exploring old logging roads, digging around ancient mining claims. Marc had a hundred plans. He wanted to canoe the Boundary Waters, to kayak down the Labrador coast, to fish in Peru. They snowboarded the Wasatch, followed wolf packs in Yellowstone's backcountry. They spent long weekends in Utah's Canyonlands, in Wyoming's Red Desert Haystacks looking for fossils. The rough country was their emotional center.

But it wasn't all joy; sometimes the adventures went to vinegar—once when the snow came in mid-October, four feet of dry powder on bare ground, snow so insubstantial they sank through it until their skis grated on rock.

"*Neige poudreuse.* Give it a few days to settle and make a base," he said. But it stayed cold and didn't pack, didn't settle, and that was it. The wind blew it around, wore it out. No more came in November, December, half of January. They were crazy with cabin fever, longing for snow. When Biff stopped by for the rent, he predicted, through a mouthful of chewing tobacco, a thousand-year drought.

"Happened before," he said. "Ask any Anasazi."

Then a line of storms moved in from the Pacific. Heavy snow and torrents of wind piled up seven-foot drifts. When they ran outside to load the skis and test the snow they could feel the tension, deep smothered sounds below indicating basal shifts.

"Today, no off *piste,*" said Marc. "And we won't even try the trails. The old skid road is probably safe enough."

On the drive up the mountain it began to snow again, and they passed men straining to push a truck out of the ditch. They crawled along in whiteout conditions.

They started skiing up the old logging road but in less than twenty minutes found it blocked by an ocean of broken snow. Looking up the east slope of the hill they could see the avalanche track, sack-shaped like the gut of a deer.

"Not good," said Marc. "No point going any farther. There's that terrain trap past the bridge." They went home, Marc saying it was likely they could be called for avalanche rescue.

A violent wind battered the trailer half the night, the electric lights flickering. But the next morning the sky was milky blue. Marc squinted at it and sighed. They waited. By eleven the skin of cloud thickened. The left hand of the storm fell on them like a dropped rock. Marc's cell phone uttered an incongruous meadowlark call.

TESTIMONY OF THE DONKEY

"Yes. Yes. Leaving now," he said. Search and Rescue needed them. He reminded Catlin to put her radio transceiver in her jacket zip pocket.

"So we won't be part of the problem." On the way he said that Ed Glide had remarked that the storm had brought out hundreds of people, who knew why? Well, because it had been a dry winter.

Catlin knew why. It was more than a dry winter. There was something about skiing in storms that thrilled certain people—climbers of dangerous rock at night, kayakers in ice-choked rivers, hikers who could not resist battering wind and hail.

At the trailhead excited people rushed around in the falling snow, shouting teenage snowboarders with huge packs on their backs, parents bellowing "Get back here" at their children, skiers slipping through the trees, all disappearing into the bludgeoning white.

Ed Glide, beard as coarse as the stuffing in antique chair seats, dark nostrils reminding one of the open doors of a two-car garage, was standing in front of the billboard trail map using a ski pole as a pointer. The fresh rescue group listened, stamped around to keep their feet warm. Ed was talking about the lost snowmobiler rescued at dawn, naked and curled up under a tree.

"There's a shitload of snow in the backcountry," he said. "And there's six damn kids on the Miner's trail. Snowshoes. They headed out this morning with one of the daddies to have a winter cookout at Horse Lake. There's that big cornice over the open slope along there. I doubt any of them's got enough sense to—" He had not finished the sentence when they all heard the heavy roar to the southwest. Even through the light snow they could see a vast cloud rising.

"Fuck!" shouted Ed. "That's it. Let's go! Go!"

A mile along the trail they met two of the boys on snowshoes, stumbling along and repeatedly falling, red faces clotted with

157

snow and frozen tears. The gasping boys said the group had almost reached Horse Lake when Mr. Shelman said the snow was too deep for a cookout and they turned back. They had barely recrossed the bottom of the open slope when the avalanche came. The others were under the snow.

The search crew spent the rest of the day looking for signs of survivors, probing, shoveling. None of the boys or Mr. Shelman had carried a transceiver. Distraught parents came postholing to the site and some of them brought the family dog. Someone found a mitten. The search went on through the night. It took two days to dig out the bodies, and forever to get over the sense of failure and loss.

"Cookout! What a fiasco," said Marc. "Poor little kids." He meant the two survivors, already stained with guilt at being alive.

Their best times were always their explorations into the remnants of the vanishing wild. They treasured discovering new country. She thought sometimes that they were seeing the end of the old world. She knew Marc felt it too. They were in such harmony that they had never had an argument until the lettuce fight.

They were leaving the next morning on a ten-day hike in the Old Bison range. The Jade trail had been closed for years but Marc relished the plan for an end run around the Forest Service. It was their practice to have a big dinner the night before they started an adventure, and then to eat sparingly in the wild, the feast a kind of Carnival before Lent. A little hunger, said Marc, makes the mind sharp. Catlin bought tomatoes, a head of lettuce, fillets of halibut at the local market. It was Marc's turn to make dinner. He was making aloko, an African dish of bananas cooked in palm oil with chile to accompany the fried halibut. And, of course, her salad.

Before he started cooking he took off his shirt, more efficient, he said, than putting on an apron. She knew it was because he didn't like the only apron in the house, a fire-engine red thing her mother had given her for a silly present. She said he would be burned by spattering grease. She said she didn't want to find chest hairs clinging to the lettuce.

"You worry too much," he said. The oily smell of frying banana spread through the trailer.

She sorted gear for the trip. Why did he still prefer those antique primitivo boots studded with hobnails? "Do you want a beer while you make the salad?"

"Isn't there any of that white wine left? Whatever it was." He was cutting a red onion—the slices too thick. If he was so continental why couldn't he cut an onion properly? She found an opened bottle of the wine in the refrigerator, poured him a glass and stood watching as he finished slicing, waved the knife with a flourish and began hacking the lettuce.

"You didn't wash it," she said. "And you're supposed to tear the leaves, not cut them."

"Babes, it's a clean lettuce, no dirt. Why wash it? Of course I would prefer a nice little endive, some mesclun, but what we've got is a big, tasteless, hard head of lettuce like a green cannonball. It deserves to be cut." There was no doubt that he despised iceberg lettuce.

"Well, that's all they had. It came from California. Who knows if they sprayed it, or whether the one who picked it had a disease or TB or peed on it?" Her voice spiraled upward. Catlin was inclined to an organic, vegetarian diet, a taste first professed when she was in her teens and designed to annoy her meat-and-potatoes parents, a diet even more difficult to uphold in beef-more-beef-and-potatoes Wyoming. She had considered herself sophisticated in food preferences until Marc. And although she usually gave in to him on whatever main dish he proposed, she insisted on the salad.

"Does everything have to be antiseptic? Does everything have to be done your way? It's only a salad, agreed, it is not a very good salad as we have only the most wretched of ingredients, but I'm making it, and you're eating it." He, of course, would sniffily ignore the salad, gobble the bananas and chile heaped on the fish.

"Oh no. I'm not eating that salad. It's probably full of hairs."

He threw down the knife in exasperation.

There were a few more verbal jabs and then suddenly they were in a shouting match about fried bananas, Africa, Mexico, immigration policy, farm labor, olive trees, California. She said he was not only a filthy lettuce nonwasher but a foreign creep who would probably eat caterpillars. He was a freeloader (he was occasionally short on his share of the rent) and he couldn't even make a simple salad. He certainly didn't know how to slice an onion. And why wear those stupid hobnail boots that made him look like a nineteenth-century Matterhorn guide? Maybe he'd like a pair of lederhosen for his birthday? He said he *had* eaten caterpillars in Africa and they were packed with protein and tasty, that the boots had belonged to his grandfather who had been a climber on serious Himalayan expeditions after the Second World War, that she had become controlling, headstrong, egotistical, provincial and unpleasant. Then came accusations of sexual failure and repulsive habits, of ex-lovers, of cheating and lying, the horrible wholesome flax-seed cereal she favored, his addiction to smelly cheeses and bread that had to be made because it could not be bought, and again the wretched hobnail boots. It was less argument than bitter testimony, as when, on the last night of Carneval in some towns in rural Spanish Galicia, a man presents the *testamento,* the rhymed and furious catalog of the village's sins in the past year, and fictionally apportions the body parts of a donkey to fit the sins. He had told her about this, and now he awarded her the donkey's flatulent gut as most expressive of her raving.

Hundreds of irritations and grievances each had kept closeted spouted from the volcanoes of their injured and insulted egos. Marc threw the salad bowl on the floor, the onion slices rolling on their broad edges. She threw his shirt in the salad. She poured olive oil on the shirt and said if he liked olive oil so much, why, here was plenty of it. She raced to the stove, seized the frying pan and dumped the banana-chile mess in the sink. When he tried to stop her she delivered him a head-ringing slap. She screamed imprecations but he was suddenly very quiet. The expression on his face was peculiar and familiar; anger and—yes, pleasure.

Then he recovered and as if to goad her began again. "You American bitch!" he said, almost conversationally, but his voice sharpening with each word. "You and this constipated place of white, narrow-minded Republicans with the same right-wing opinions. There's no diversity, there's no decent food, there's no conversation, there's no ideas, there's nothing except the scenery. And the Alps have more beautiful scenery than the Rockies." He folded his arms and waited.

"Well, it's good to hear what you really think. Why don't you clear out. Go fuck old fat-legs Julia!" Her voice was a diabolic screech. Yet even as she yelled she was embarrassed by the florid theatricality of the scene. And he wondered how could she know anything about Julia. He had never mentioned her. Julia was his mother.

His lips infolded, he stalked through the rooms collecting his remaining clothes, his books, the maligned hobnail boots, his GPS unit and climbing gear, his skis, his African mask collection, coldly packing everything into his truck. He said nothing while she continued to make caustic taunts. Striding through the kitchen he slipped on the olive oil and nearly fell. Humiliation deepened his anger. She noticed the bandage on his left hand was stained with pus and blood. A few days earlier, trying to strike flakes from a gleaming lump of obsidian Ed Glide had given him, he had driven a sliver deep into his hand. It must be infected, she thought with malicious joy.

The last thing he did was to rip down her poster of Big Train Johnson, the centerpiece of her Shrine to Idaho Baseball, showing the pitcher just after he'd hurled the ball, right-hand knuckles bent, an expression of mild curiosity on his plain face. Marc glared at her. It seemed to her he was presenting his face to get smacked again. She didn't move and abruptly he left.

Through the window she saw him get in his truck and drive away. South. Toward Denver, where, as he had said, there was more than one skin color, a cultural mix and an international airport.

She cleaned up the salad with his ruined shirt, crammed the greasy mess into a trash bag. Slowly she calmed and a brilliant thought came; she would hike the Jade trail without him. She didn't need him.

She slept only a few hours, waking twice to the knowledge that they had broken up. She got up with the first light, boiled a dozen eggs—good hiking trip food—and packed the Jeep. The phone rang as she was carrying out the last load.

"Catlin," he said quietly. "I've got two tickets to Athens on a flight tomorrow morning. I'm going to fight the wildfires in Greece. Will you come?"

"I've got other plans." She hung up, then pulled out the phone cord. She tossed her watch and cell phone in the silverware drawer and rushed out the door. Somewhere along the way, not from *him,* she had learned that discarding the technology sharpened the senses, led to deeper awareness.

On the road driving north she felt she was once again in her own life. For miles she listened to music by groups he despised, reveling in the sense of liberation. He favored Alpha Blondy or monotonous talking-drum music on long drives. She could not stop thinking about the breakup, and after a while even her favorite tunes seemed to develop talking-drum backgrounds. Silence was better. She recalled the strangely pleased expression on Marc's face after she hit him, familiar but impossible to place in context.

It was dusk when she reached the town at the edge of the Big Bison National Forest. She found a motel. She did not want to miss the signless trailhead in evening gloom. The wind came up in the night, occasionally lifting her from sleep. Each time she stretched, thinking how wonderful it was to have the whole bed to herself. It was not until the morning that she discovered she had left the topo map back at the trailer in her haste to get out. At the local hardware store she found another, compiled from aerial photographs taken in 1958. It was better than the forgotten map as the Jade trail was clearly marked.

She found some paper in the glove compartment—the receipt for the last oil change—and with an old pencil stub that had rolled around on the dash for a year she scrawled her name, "Jade Trail" and the date and left it on the seat.

Even in broad daylight the abandoned trail was difficult to find. Years before, the Forest Service had uprooted the sign and blocked off the entrance with fallen pines and boulders. Young lodgepole had grown up to shoulder height. The map showed that six miles north the trail flanked an unnamed mountain, then curled around half a dozen small glacier lakes. Marc had planned to fish those lakes. A disturbing thought came to her. He might not go to Athens but return to the trailer and find her gone, notice that all her camping gear was missing. He would know immediately that she had come up to hike the trail without him. He would follow her. She would have to watch and dodge.

The first mile was unpleasant; the trail was rocky and the soil a fine dust half an inch deep. It was clear that many hikers ignored the "Trail Closed" legend on the forest map and ventured up it for a mile or two before turning back. They had marked their passage with broken branches which clawed her arms.

Gradually the head-high trees disappeared as the trail led into the old forest. She walked soundlessly on the thick needle duff. The trail bent and opened onto views of forested slopes, showing thousands of deep red-orange trees killed by the mountain pine beetle infestation and drought. In open areas the trail was choked with seedlings reclaiming the ground. The young trees looked healthy and green, still untouched by the beetles. She wondered if the world was seeing the last of the lodgepole forests. If Marc had been with her they would have talked about this. The memory of his stained bandage came to her. He had determined to learn how to make stone projectile points. They had talked about prehistoric stone tools, and when he told her their edges were only a few microns thick and sharper than razors, she idly wondered aloud why terrorists did not arm themselves with chert knives that would escape airport detection.

"That's stupid," he said.

After several miles of level ground the trail began to climb and twist in a steep stairway of roots and rocks. Snowmelt had scoured it out to slick earth packed around bony flints. Around noon the trail broke into an explosion of wildflowers—columbine, penstemon, beautiful Clarkia, chickweed and Indian paintbrush.

Delighted by the alpine meadow and a few banks of snow packed into clefts on the north sides of slopes, she looked down at a small lake. The scene was exquisitely beautiful. But even here it was not as cool as she had expected. The sun was strong and a cloud of gnats and mosquitoes warped around her in elliptical flight. She ate her lunch sitting in the shade of a giant boulder. She did not miss Marc.

She looked west at Buffalo Hunter, the highest peak in the range. Its year-round snow cover was gone and the peak stood obscenely bare, a pale grey summit quivering in radiant heat. Rock that had not seen sunlight in hundreds of years lay exposed. Another hot, dry summer, the sky filling with wind-torn clouds and lightning but no rain. Occasionally a few drops rattled the air before the clouds dragged them away. Next month the Arizona monsoon would move in with blessed rain, but now the flatland below was parched, the grasses seeded out and withered to a brittle tan wire that cracked underfoot. In the mountains the heat was almost as intense as at lower elevations, and the earth lifeless gravel.

By late afternoon she was tired and reckoned she had hiked thirteen or fourteen miles. The Jade trail ran for another sixty-odd miles and came out on a dead trailhead near a mining ghost town. From the ruins to the main road was another four or five miles. She was sure she could do it easily in ten days. She pitched the little tent beside an unnamed glacier-melt lake. As she ate her hydrated tomato soup she watched trout rise to an evening hatch, the perfect circles spreading outward on the water, coalescing with other spreading circles. The setting sun illuminated the millions of flying insects as a glittering haze over the lake. Marc would have been down there matching the evening hatch, but he was probably in Greece by now. A grey jay, remembering the good old days when hikers had scattered bread crusts and potato chips along the trail, watched expectantly. She crumbled a cracker for him and gave him a name—Johnson, in honor of Big Train Johnson. The day left her a sky veneered with pink pearl, the black ridge against it serrated with pine tops like obsidian spear blades. She was not afraid of the dark and sat up listening to the night sounds until the last liquid smear of light in the west was gone. There was no moon.

She had slept on a stone and wakened stiff and aching in the vague morning. As soon as the sun came up the mountains began to heat, the few remaining snowdrifts melting to feed the gurgling rivulets that twisted through the alpine meadows. The snow patches lay in fantastic shapes, maps of remote archipelagoes, splatters of spilled yogurt, dirty legs, swan wings. There was no wind and the gnats and mosquitoes were bad enough that she slathered on insect repellent. She limbered up with a few bends and stretches, boiled water for tea, ate two of the boiled eggs in her pack and started off again. The eggs had picked up insect repellent from her fingers and the nasty smarting taste stayed in her mouth for a long time.

She hiked past half a dozen small lakes dimpled with rings from rising trout and thought of Marc. She could hear but not see a rushing stream under the willows, a stream that cascaded from the high melting snowbanks. Obscurant mountain willow grew thick wherever the water trickled. The shallow lakes, the color of brown khaki and denim blue, reflected the peaks and shrinking snowfields above. Some lakes were a profound, saturated blue shading out from tawny boulders at the edge to depths where the big fish rested in the coolest water. The waterlines marking shore boulders told that the lake levels once had been four or five feet higher.

The trail slanted steadily upward and was so badly overgrown that long sections melted into the general mountain terrain.

Twice she lost it and had to scramble to a high point to see its continuation. She was close now to the height of land where the trail would run above tree line for seven or eight miles before starting down the west slope. This was country where great shelves and masses of shadowed rock displayed exquisite lichen worlds. She knew the lichen chemical factories broke down the rock into soil, some of them fanning across the stone like a stain, nitrogen-loving hot orange lichen where foxes had urinated. Marc had said once that lichens might have been the earth's first plants, that over millions of years they had converted the world's rock covering into the soil that allowed life; the lichens they saw were still devouring the mountains. On their hikes they had seen lichens in hundreds of shapes and colors—flames, antlers, specks and fiery dots, potato chips, caviar, blobs of jelly, corn kernels, green hair, tiny felt mittens, skin diseases, Lilliputian pink-rimmed cups. They always told each other that they were going to learn the lichens, and then, back home, never did.

The rocks themselves, wreathed to their knees in a foam of columbine blossom, were too beautiful to look at for long. One massive soft red rock, as large as three houses, was splotched with pea green lichen. She scratched at the lichen with her fingernail, but it was impervious to abrasion. Flowering plants grew on the rock's small ledges and shelves. This perfection of color and place, too rare and too much to absorb, induced a great sadness; she did not know why and thought it might be rooted in a primordial sense of the spiritual. In this wild place there were no signs of humans except the high mumble of an occasional jet. The solitude provoked existential thoughts, and she regretted the argument with Marc which fell steadily toward the importance of a fuzz of dust. But she was not unhappy to be alone. "Puts things in perspective, right, Johnson?" she said to the grey jay who was following her.

* * *

On the next day around noon she reached a church-size rock about a hundred feet from a tan lake, really more cliff than rock, an interlocking system of glistening pink house-size chunks of granite cracked and fractured into blocks and shelves so huge a few young pines had found enough soil to keep them alive. Their forcing roots would split the rock in time. The ground between the cliff and the lake was littered with a talus of fallen boulders. A few miles away bare scree-covered slopes protruded from the gnarled krummholz, marking the trail's maximum height. She did not want to hike up there in late afternoon, to be forced by darkness to camp in the lightning zone. Even now torn grey clouds slid over the naked peaks. The map showed the tallest as "Tolbert Mountain." The sun was halfway down the western sky. She would quit for the day and camp here. She eased off her backpack and let it drop heavily to the trail. It made a hard clank. The trail here crossed a vast sheet of granite half a mile wide. To be free from the familiar weight was a luxury and she stretched.

High up on the pink cliff she thought she saw writing—initials and a date? Early miners and travelers had left their marks everywhere. She decided to scramble up and see what it was; maybe Jim Bridger, John Fremont or Jedediah Smith, or some other important historical figure. She felt a bitter dart of loss, like a thorn under the fingernail, that Marc wasn't with her. He would have shouted with joy at this beautiful trail and the pristine lakes, and he would have climbed directly to the inscription on the rock.

The bottom third of the cliff was a rubble of fallen breakstone encrusted with the nubby fabric of grey lichen. Then came fifty feet of climbable clean granite that gave way abruptly to an almost perpendicular wall of glinting stone bristling with jutting blocks.

She was determined to get near enough to read the inscription, for she was sure the marks were weathered letters.

The climb was more difficult than it looked. Several stones at the bottom wobbled a little, but so near the ground they seemed hardly a concern. Above them was a tiny trail formed by rain and snow runoff snaking down from an upper jam of more broken blocks, just wide enough for her foot. She inched up the tiny path as far as the lowest block and managed to claw her way around its side, not looking down. Now she was close enough to make out the letters daubed in black paint, JOSÉ 1931. Not a famous explorer after all—just some old Mexican sheepherder. So much for that.

Getting down was surprisingly awkward. Small rocks turned and slid beneath her feet. In one place she had to slide down a rough incline that rucked her pants uncomfortably up into her crotch. She was in a hurry to set up camp as soon as she got down. This would be the night to break out the pint of rum, maybe mix it with the bottle of cranberry juice she had lugged for days. She craved the thirst-quenching acidity.

Near the bottom she jumped eighteen inches onto the top stone in the jackstraw jumble. The stone swiveled as though it were on ball bearings. Her foot plunged down into the gap between it and another rock and with her weight off it, once more the huge stone shifted, pinning her leg. At first, while she struggled, she ignored the pain and thought of her situation as a temporary obstacle. Then, unable to move the rock or to pull out of its grip, she understood she was trapped.

It took a long time—several minutes—for her to grasp the situation because she was so furious. On the climb up that same block had shifted slightly with a stony rasp as though clearing its throat. Because it was less than two feet from the ground she had considered it inconsequential. She had not taken care. If Marc had been with her he would have said something like "Watch out for this rock." And if Marc was with her he could push or pry up the rock long enough for her to pull her leg out. If Marc was with her. If anyone was with her. She certainly knew the stupidity of hiking alone. She had climbed up there because that was what Marc would have done. So, in a causative way, he was there.

She kept trying to pull the rapidly swelling leg free. The rock pressed against her calf and knee. She could slightly move her ankle and foot. That was the only good news. As a child she had learned that those who did not give up lived, while those who quit trying died. And sometimes those who did not give up died anyway. She thought of her chances. If Marc went back to the trailer he would find the forgotten map on the kitchen table. He would see her camping gear was missing. He would know she was on the Jade trail and he would come. Unless, said her dark, inner voice, unless he was in Greece on some fire line. And if he was in Greece, would Forest Service personnel notice her jeep sitting there day after day? Would they see her note on the front seat, now six days old, and come looking? Those were her chances: to free herself; for Marc to come; for a Forest Service search and rescue. There was one more slender possibility. Another hiker or fisherman might take the closed trail. In the meantime she was mad thirsty. Her backpack was on the trail where she had dropped it, but because it was behind her she could not even see it. In it were the cranberry juice, food, the tiny stove, matches, a signal mirror—everything. In frustration she heaved at the rock which did not move.

As twilight advanced she cried angrily, raging at the tiny misstep that might cost her everything. Her tongue stuck to the roof of her dry mouth. Eventually, leaning against the cooling rock, she fell into a half doze, starting awake many times. Her trapped leg was numb. Thirst and the cold mountain air fastened onto her like leeches. Her neck ached, and she pulled her shoulders forward.

She shivered, wrapped her arm around herself, but the shivering intensified until she was racked with deep, clenching shudders. Possible scenes rolled through her head. Could she get so cold the trapped leg would shrink enough to let her pull it out? She pulled again, the fiftieth time, and could feel the edge of the huge stone pressing down on the top of her kneecap. Could she summon the strength to pull the leg relentlessly up even if the edge of the rock cut or crushed the kneecap? She tried until the pain overwhelmed. The effort eased the shuddering for a few minutes, but soon her muscles were clenching violently again. She prayed for morning, remembered how hot it had been every day. She thought if she could just get warm she would get back some strength, and if she had water, after she drank, surely she could get the leg out. She could pour water—if she had it—down her leg and perhaps the water would provide enough lubrication to let her get free. As she thought about this she realized that urine might both warm her and lubricate the trapped leg. But the warmth was fleeting and any lubrication went unnoticed by the rock, which had now passed from inanimate object to malevolent personality.

Between shuddering spasms she fell into tiny snatches of sleep just a few seconds in duration. Finally the stars paled and the sky turned the color of crabapple jelly.

"Come on, come on," she begged the sun, which rose with interminable slowness. At last sunlight struck the ridge to the west, but she was still in cold shadow. An hour passed. She could hear birds. One perched on the edge of the cruel rock just out of her reach. If she could seize it she would bite its head off and drink the blood. But the air was slowly warming even if the sun rays were still not touching the rock. Her leg felt like a great pounding column. At last the blessed sun fell across her body, and gradually the shuddering slowed. The wonderful heat relaxed her and she nodded off for long minutes. But each time she snapped awake her thirst was a disease, enflaming every pore of her body, swelling her throat. She could feel her fat tongue thickening.

The sun's warmth, so pleasant and grateful, became heat, burning her exposed arms, her neck and face. The eagles screamed overhead. By noon her smarting skin and clamorous thirst over-shadowed the injured leg. Her eyes were scratchy and hot, and she had to blink to see the distant scree cones that seemed to pulse in the heat. By sunset those naked peaks had changed to heaps of glowing metal shavings. Several times throughout the day she imagined Marc's approach and called out to him. A fox ran up toward the snowbank with something in its mouth.

Now she took new stock of the object that was imprisoning her. It was an irregularly shaped block of granite roughly three feet long and two feet high, the top a sloping table with a scooped declivity a foot or so long and perhaps two inches deep in the center. She could just reach the declivity with her fingers.

The sun notched down the sky, changing the rock shadows. A curious marmot ran to the top of the adjacent rock and stared at her, ran down beneath it, reappeared from a different direction. Johnson, the grey jay, flew in and out of her vision so often he seemed a floater. There was nothing to see but Johnson, the marmot, the dots of black lichen, the eagles in the sky. There was only one thing to think about. Then, as the sun declined, there was another: night and cold.

The rock lost its heat slowly but with cruel inevitability. The sun crashed below the horizon and immediately a stream of chill air flowed down from the snow slopes. At first the coolness felt good on her burned skin, but within the hour she was shivering. She knew what was coming and so did her body, which seemed to brace itself. Far overhead she heard the drone of a small plane engine. Her mind raced to think of a way she could signal a plane the next day. She had a reflecting mirror in her backpack. If only she had worn her watch; if only she had brought the cell phone. If only she was not alone. If only she and Marc had not quarreled. If only he would come. Now. She thought that the sounds of his approach she had imagined during the day must have been a fox raiding her backpack. The night dragged and she dozed woozily for longer periods, minutes instead of seconds, bent over at the waist, for the rock made a kind of slanting table at just the height to cripple cotton pickers and short-row hoers. The leg alternated between numbness and throbbing.

The morning was bitterly familiar. She felt she had been trapped here since infancy. Nothing before the rock was real. She was a mouse in a mousetrap. Everything was the same, the brightening sky, the yearning for the sun's heat. Her tongue filled her mouth and her fingers were stiff. She mistook the grey jay, Johnson, standing two feet away from her on the far edge of the rock, for a wolf. The dull peaks at the height of land were very like monstrous ocean waves, and she could see them swell and roll. The surface of the rock holding her in its grasp was fine-grained, lustrous, dotted with pinprick lichens. The sky bent over the rock. Something smelled bad. Was it her leg or her urine-soaked jeans. Again her drying eyes went to the ocean waves, back down to the rock, to Johnson, who had now taken the guise of the sleeve of her grey chenille bathrobe, to the surface of the rock, to her cramping hands and back again to the naked scree slopes. She had not known that dying could be so boring. She fell asleep for moments and dreamed about the granite mousetrap, built with such care by an unknown stonemason. She dreamed that her father had pulled up a chair nearby. He said that her leg was going to wither and drop off, but that she could make a nice crutch from a small pine and hop back down the trail. She dreamed that a rare butterfly landed on the rock and an entomologist who looked like Marc came for it, easily lifting the stone from her leg and showing her the special mountain wheelchair he had brought to get her down the slopes.

When she snapped back to consciousness the sky hunched over the rock, the slopes, the high snowbanks oozed and sagged, undulating in rhythm with the bald knobs. Time itself writhed and fluttered. Johnson the jay was making thick booming sounds such as no bird had ever before produced. He was a drum, an empty oil barrel on which someone was beating a message, a talking drum. She almost understood. The sun seemed to go up and down like a yo-yo, splitting her eyes with light, then disappearing. Something was happening. She could just make out tiny lichens, transparent, hopping on the stone, on the backs of her hands, on her head and arms. She opened her mouth and the lichens became rain falling on her roasted tongue. Immediately she felt a surge of gratification and pleasure. She cupped her hands to catch the rain but they were too stiff. The rain poured off her hair, dripped from the end of her nose, soaked her shirt, filled the declivity in the top of the rock with blessed water that she could not quite reach.

She drank the downpour, feeling strength and reason return. When the storm moved away her head was clearer. The hard blue sky pressed down and the sun began to pull in the moisture like someone reeling in a hose. She managed to get her shirt off and by making a feeble toss at the water-filled declivity, which held several cups of water, landed one sleeve in the precious puddle. She pulled it toward her and sucked the moisture from the sleeve, repeating the gesture until she had swallowed it all. Not far away she could hear one of the tiny mountain streams rattling through the stones. Her mind was lucid enough to realize that the rain might have only postponed one of the eternal verities. She could see other thunderheads to the east, but nothing to the northwest, the direction of the prevailing wind. The grey jay was not in her sight line.

She had sopped the declivity dry with her shirt, and now she pulled it back on against the burning sun. The gravelly soil had swallowed the rain. There was nothing to do but squint against the glittering world. The cycle started once more. Within an hour her thirst, which, before the storm, had begun to dim, returned with ferocity. Her entire body, her fingernails, her inner ears, the ends of her greasy hair, screamed for water. She bored holes in the sky looking for more rain.

In the night lightning teased in the distance but no more rain fell. The top of the imprisoning rock became a radiant plain under a sliver of ancient moonlight.

By morning the temporary jolt of strength and clarity was gone. She felt as though electricity was shooting up through the rock and into her torso, needles and pins and the numbness that followed was almost welcome, although she dimly knew what it meant. Apparitions swarmed from the snowbanks above, fountains and dervishes, streaming spigots, a helicopter with a water-slide, a crowd of garishly dressed people reaching down, extending their hands to her. All day a desiccating hot wind blew and made her nearly blind. She could not close her eyes. The sun was horrible and her tongue hung in her mouth like a metal bell clapper, clacking against her teeth. Her hands and arms had changed to black and grey leather, a kind of lichen. Her ears swarmed with rattling and buzzing and her shirt seemed made of a stiff metal that chafed her lizard skin.

In the long struggle to get her painful shirt off, through the buzzing in her ears, through her cracking skin she heard Marc. He was wearing the hobnail boots and coming up the trail behind her. This was no illusion. She fought to clear her senses and heard it clearly, the hobnail boots sharply click-click-clicking up the granite section of trail. She tried to call his name, but "Marc" came out as a guttural roar, "*Maaaa* . . .," a thick and frightening primeval sound. It startled the doe and her half-grown fawns behind her, and they clattered down the trail, black hooves clicking over the rock out of sight and out of hearing.

Tits-Up in a Ditch

Her mother had been knockout beautiful and no good and Dakotah had heard this from the time she recognized words. People said that Shaina Lister with aquamarine eyes and curls the shining maroon of waterbirch bark had won all the kiddie beauty contests and then had become the high school slut, knocked up when she was fifteen and cutting out the day after Dakotah was born, slinking and wincing, still in her hospital johnny, down the back stairs of Mercy Maternity to the street, where one of her greasy pals picked her up and headed west for Los Angeles. It was the same day television evangelist Jim Bakker, a found-out and confessed adulterer, resigned from his Praise the Lord money mill, his fall mourned by Bonita Lister, Shaina's mother. Bonita's husband, Verl, blamed the television for Shaina's wildness and her hatred of the ranch.

"She seen it was okay on the teevee and so she done it." He said he wanted to get rid of the set but Bonita said there was no sense in locking up the horse after the barn burned down. Although Verl deplored the corrupting influence of television he said that since he was paying for the electricity he might as well get some use out of the thing. And saw danger, mystery, secrets and humiliation.

Verl and Bonita Lister were in their late thirties and stuck with the baby. If it had been a boy, Verl said, letting the words squeeze out around his roll-yer-own, he could have helped with the chores when he got to size. And inherited the ranch, was the implied finish to the sentence. Verl had named Dakotah after his homesteading great-grandmother, born in the territory, married and widowed and married again only after she had proved up on the place and the deed was in her name and in her hand. Later she was known for ridding the family of fleas by boiling the wash in a mixture of sheep dip and kerosene. In a day when the mourning period for a husband was two or three years and for a wife was three months, she had worn black for her first husband an insulting six weeks, then taken up a homestead claim. Verl treasured a photograph showing her with the precious deed, standing in front of her neat clapboarded house, a frowsy white dog leaning against her checkered skirt. She held one hand behind her back, and Verl said this was because she smoked a pipe. Dakotah was almost sure she could see a wisp of smoke curling up, but Bonita said it was dust raised by the wind. Since that pioneer time the country had become trammeled and gnawed, stippled with cattle, coal mines, oil wells and gas rigs, striated with pipelines. The road to the ranch had been named Sixteen Mile, though no one was sure what that distance signified.

Bottle-blond Bonita (her great-grandfather had been a squaw man and black hair was in the genes) made an early grandmother. Ranch-raised and trained, she counted the grandchild as a difficulty that had to be met. She was used to praising thankless work as the right and good way, but what she was going to do without Jim Bakker's exhortation and encouragement she didn't know. First, an impaired husband, the endless labor and (sometimes forced) good humor that was expected of women, then a bad-girl daughter, and now the bad girl's baby to raise. Verl Lister was burden enough. He could not run the ranch alone and they often had to ask their neighbors to throw together and help out. Of course it was because he had been a wild boy in his youth, had rodeoed hard, a bareback rider who suffered falls, hyperextensions and breaks that had bloomed into arthritis and aches as he aged. A trampling had broken his pelvis and legs so that now he walked with the slinking crouch of a bagpipe player. She could not fault him for ancient injuries, and remembered him as the straight-backed, curly-headed young man with beautiful eyes sitting on his horse, back straight as a metal fence post. But a man, she thought, was supposed to endure pain silently, cowboy up and not bitch about it all day long. She, too, had arthritis in her left knee, but she suffered in silence.

Throughout the 1980s it was a puzzle where all the able-bodied labor had gone. During the energy boom, oil companies had sucked up Wyoming boys, offering high wages that no rancher, not even Wyatt Match, the county's richest cattleman, could pay. When the bust came there were still no ranch hands for hire. "You'd think," said Verl, "with all them oil companies pullin out there'd be fifty guys on every corner lookin for work." But the hands, after their taste of roustabout money, had followed the dollar away from Wyoming.

Verl was a trash rancher, said Wyatt Match, oyster eyes sliding around behind his gold-rimmed lenses that darkened in sunlight, and not so much because his land was overgrazed, but because there were fences down and gates hanging by one hinge, binder twine everywhere, rusting machinery in the pastures, and because the Listers' kitchen table was covered with a vinyl tablecloth showing the Last Supper. There was an old sedan with the hood up in one of the irrigation ditches. A defunct electric stove rested on the front porch. The Lister cows roamed the roads, constantly suffered accidents, drowning in the creek in spring flood, bogging in mud pots that came from nowhere.

Spring was the hardest time, the weather alternating between blizzards and Saharan heat. On a snow-whipped evening, Dakotah setting the table for supper, Verl said a cow who had tried to climb a steep, wet slope that apparently slid out from under her, had landed on her back in the ditch.

"Had me some luck today. Goddamn cow got herself tits-up in the ditch couple days ago. Dead, time I found her," he said in a curiously satisfied tone, squinting through faded lashes, winking his eyes, the same aquamarine color as those of the wayward Shaina.

"Not every man would say that is luck," said Bonita wearily. She pulled at a stray thread protruding from the leg seam of her pink slacks. It was an impractical color but she believed pastels projected freshness and youth. She went to the sink, stepping over Bum, Verl's ancient heeler crippled by cow kicks, and began scrubbing out the only pot large enough to boil potatoes in quantity, a pot she used several times a day.

"It is, in a way of speakin."

She couldn't puzzle that one out, even if she had had the time. With Verl it was one thing after another. He went into the national forest to cut wood every fall, and she knew that he someday would cut himself in half with the cranky old chain saw. She almost hoped he would.

For Verl Lister everything turned on luck, and he had experienced very little of the good kind. His secret boyhood dream had been to become a charismatic radio man meeting singing personalities, giving the news, announcing songs, describing the weather. All of this grew from a small, cheap radio he had earned as a boy selling Rosebud salve, riding ranch to ranch on an aged mare. At night, forbidden to listen past nine o'clock, he put it under the covers and turned it whisper low, listening to honey-voiced Paul Kallinger on a high-watt border station, the lonely hearts club ads, pitches for tonics and elixirs, yodeling cowboys, and, by the time he was in his teens, Wolfman Jack of scandalous sex talk and panting and howls. Yet he never wanted to be like Wolfman Jack. Kallinger was his ideal.

He had no idea how to get into the radio game, as he thought of it, and the plan faded as he grew into work on the home ranch. For fun he rode broncs, the source of his present miseries. He still kept the radio in his truck on constantly, had a radio in every room of the house despite the region's bad reception. Mostly he listened to the stations that featured songs about lost love and drinking, used car sales ads, church doings and auctions, stations that were pale imitations of the old border blasters of his youth. When NPR came to Wyoming in the 1960s, he judged it dull and hoity-toity. For him television was never as good as radio. He found that screen images were inferior to those in his mind.

Growing up, Wyatt Match had been given every advantage. He had good horses from the time he could walk, trips abroad, hand-tooled boots. He went to an eastern prep school and then the University of Pennsylvania. After graduation he came back to Wyoming with one or two ideas about agricultural progress and tried too soon to get into the legislature when the times favored conservative, frugal ranchers as political leaders, not spendthrift rich men, a label his father's private golf course had burned into an envious population. Over the years he had become a sharp-horned archconservative with a hard little mind like a diamond chip. After his youthful start flirting with useless ideas sown by the eastern professors, he had dedicated himself to maintaining the romantic heritage of the nineteenth-century ranch, Wyoming's golden time. Descended from Irish stock, he had a milky skin that flamed with sunburn, and his ginger hair had turned a saintly white. His pride was a blue neon sign—MATCH RANCH—near his monstrous post-and-lintel gate large enough to be the torii of a Shinto shrine. After years of trying he had finally made it into the state legislature. Local people were used to seeing his dusty Silverado bulge out onto the road and pass them on the right, throwing up a storm of gravel.

There was a tinge of superiority in all that he said, even in meaningless comments about weather. Match seemed to indicate that blizzards, windstorms, icy roads and punishing hail were for other people; he moved in a cloud of different, special weather. In the days when he was trying to push his way into the legislature with his radical ideas, a well-respected older rancher took him aside and told him, stressing his words, that Wyoming was *fine just the way it was*. Gradually he learned the truth of that statement.

His political value increased after he married Debra Gale Sunchley, a fifth-generation Wyoming ranch woman, a hard worker with a built-in capacity for endurance who dressed in crease-ironed jeans, boots and an old Carhartt jacket. The first Sunchley had come to Wyoming with the 11th Ohio Volunteers to fight Indians after the Civil War. Stationed at Post Greasewood on the North Platte, he deserted, hid out with a Finn coal mining family in Carbon and eventually married one of the daughters, Johanna Haapakoski.

Debra Gale Sunchley Match was secretary-treasurer of the Cow Belles, and member of the Christian Women's Book Circle. The Book Circle, always striving to do good and become better, favored memoirs by old cowboys and ranchers who personified grit and endurance. Debra Gale had read no more than ten books in her life but knew she had as much right as anyone to give her opinion. After Wyatt divorced her to marry Carol Shovel, whom he had met on a California golf vacation, Debra Gale and her brother Tuffy Sunchley stayed on as joint ranch managers. Match built his ex-wife her own house on the property, a simple one-story ranch with a big shed for her nine dogs. He paid her a wage. She was a good worker and he wasn't going to let her go.

As Dakotah grew up the Lister ranch staggered along, Bonita making ends meet, worrying about money and Verl's health. The only free time she had was kneeling at the side of the bed saying her prayers, asking for strength to go on and for her husband's well-being.

"Don't let yourself get old before your time," she said impatiently to Verl who seemed to look forward to old age. It took half an hour in the morning for him to limber up his joints. It irritated her that the child, Dakotah, had little interest in riding or rodeo, resisted 4-H meetings. Bonita could always think of some task or job for the girl, whether collecting eggs, picking over beans or discovering the section of broken fence where the cows got out. Scraping the burned toast for Verl was the most hated task. Verl insisted on toast but would not part with the money for a toaster.

"My mother made good toast on the griddle. It come already buttered," he said. Bonita often burned the toast as she tried to cook eggs and hash, forgetting the smoking bread. Dakotah rasped the charcoal into the sink with a table knife.

Once, moved by some filament of need for affection, Dakotah tried to hug Bonita, who was scrubbing potatoes in the sink. Bonita briskly shoved her away. Once in a while Dakotah wandered around the ranch on foot, usually heading for the steep pine slope with a tiny spring, the ground littered with old grey bones from a time when a mountain lion had her den beneath a fallen tree. Bonita herself never went for a walk, a wasteful dereliction of duty. She worked spring branding with the men and still managed dinner for all hands, was again on a horse at November sale time overseeing the cows prodded into cattle trucks with Swiss-cheese sides while Verl cut winter wood in the forest. Verl walked nowhere, was always in his truck when he wasn't in the reclining chair he favored. He would come into the house and sigh.

"Well, I had me some luck today," he would say in his plaintive voice.

She waited. This might be one of his slow unwinding stories that went nowhere, wasted her time.

"Filled up the gas can, got up there in the woods and damned if the can hadn't tipped over and spilled out all the gas."

Yes, it was. He was speaking in his portentous, I've-got-grave-news voice. She nodded, scraped carrots, making the orange fiber fly. She was still in her red pajama bottoms, had pushed the heifers out of the east pasture, mended a broken section of fence, got the mail, fed the bum lambs and was now cooking dinner. There had been no time to pull on a pair of jeans. She wasn't going to town anyway.

"And then I got to workin awhile and the chain broke."

"Well, you surely had problems." Once, oppressed by Verl's self-pitying complaints, she had considered poisoning him. But they carried no insurance and how she could manage alone she didn't know and gave up the idea. Then, too, she never forgot the joyous winter when they were courting, the long freezing drive in from the ranch in a truck with a broken heater to meet him at the Double Arrow Café. Her teeth chattering, she would walk from the snowy street into the wonderfully hot and noisy bar, Russ Eftink punching G5 again and again to make "Blue Bayou" play continuously, and Verl, the tough handsome cowboy, slouching across the room toward her and pulling her into the music. Into the pot went the carrots and she started on potatoes with an ancient peeler that had been in the kitchen since Verl's great-grandmother's day. The wood handle had broken away decades earlier. Most of her kitchen tools were old or broken—an egg-beater with a loose handle bolt that fell into the mixture, a chipped and rusted enamel colander, warped frying pans and spoons worn to the quick.

His voice lifted. "And my chest didn't hurt today the way it done yesterday."

"Uh-huh." She rinsed the potatoes and cubed them so they would cook faster.

"I supposed to go see her, that doctor, tomorrow mornin at ten minutes before eight. I don't know if I should now. Seein it didn't hurt today."

"Well, Verl, it might a been a matter a luck, don't you think? That it didn't hurt and you workin so hard."

He squinted at her, trying to tell if she was being sarcastic. "It's just I don't want a leave you all alone, and me dead of a heart attack," he said sanctimoniously.

She said nothing.

"So I guess I better go." It was what he'd intended to do from the beginning.

Wyatt Match thought Verl Lister's dilapidated place gave Wyoming ranchers a slob name. He personally thanked heaven that Lister was not on the main road. He often quoted Robert Frost's line "good fences make good neighbors" without understanding the poem or the differences of intent between those who made fences of stone and those who used barbed wire. He had picked the Listers to criticize, and whether it was Verl's work habits or the way he never looked straight at anyone except in the left eye, or Bonita's aqua rayon pantsuit, Wyatt Match made them out to be the county fools. In truth, Verl Lister's cows were wild and rough because they were rarely worked; they suffered parasites, hoof rot, milk fever, prolapses and hernias; they were shot by rifle and bow and arrow, they fell on tee-posts, ate wire, coughed and snuffled, fell into streams and drowned. Verl referred to Match as "him and his click. Them bastards pretty much run things the way they want." Yet if he met Match at a cattle sale or the feed store, he would smile and greet him cordially. And Match, in his turn, would say, "How'r you, Verl?" But if they crossed on the back roads in their trucks, Verl lifted three fingers in salute while Match, face bright with sun color, stared straight ahead. Pete Azkua, the grandson of a Basque sheep rancher, put it simply: *"Nahi bezala haundiak ahal bezala ttipiak,"* which he said meant the big boys do what they want, the small fry do what they can, which accounted for certain sour faces around town.

Verl resented Match, but it was Match's second wife, Carol Shovel, whom he truly detested. She was a California woman with red eyebrows and foxy hair, clothed in revealing dresses and garnished with clanking bracelets. She considered herself an authority on everything. She was a smart-mouth. No one knew why she had married Match. Of course, they said, he did have money, not from ranching, but through the Cowboy Slim Program, his father's patented weight-loss mail-order plan. Carol Match had endless recipes for Wyoming's betterment: bring back the train or start up a bus line for public transportation; invite black people and Asians to move in and improve ethnic diversity; shift the capital to Cody; make the state attractive to moviemakers and computer commuters. It got around that she had said Wyoming people were lazy. *Lazy!* Verl was outraged. Although he himself avoided as much work as he could, it was because he was half-crippled and work was bad for his heart. The whole world, except this California bitch, knew that there were no more frugal, thrifty, tough and hardworking people on the face of the earth than those in Wyoming. Work was almost holy, good physical labor done cheerfully and for its own sake, the center of each day, the node of Wyoming life. That and toughing it out when adversity struck, accepting that it was not necessary to wear a seat belt because when it was time for you to go, you went. Not being constrained by a seat belt was the pioneer spirit of freedom.

"I'd sure tell *her* where to set her empties, but you can't tell nobody like that nothin," he said to Bonita. "She is too ignorant. It would just be water off a duck's ass."

One day in the auto parts store, where Carol Match was checking to see if their order for a side window sunscreen for the restored 1948 Chevy half-ton had come in, he listened to her talk to Chet Bree behind the counter. She was wearing a tiny blue skirt with a hem just below her fatty buttocks and a silky top that showed off her robust tanned breasts.

"They have *got* to put a traffic light at that intersection. Somebody is going to get killed one day." Her bracelets rattled.

"Always been okay the way it is. Just got to be a little bit careful. People here never had no trouble with it." Bree looked at her chest for a few seconds, then looked away, then again let his gaze slide down into the cleft. Verl almost had the view of her bum.

"The place needs some new people," she said.

Verl understood that she didn't just mean importing strangers. She meant an exchange. For every ignorant California fool she brought in, a Wyoming-born native would be . . . removed. He was sure she had a list and that he was on it. Bree said nothing, and that, thought Verl, had probably got him on the list.

"Wyomin is fine just the way it is," said Verl to Bonita. "They come in here and . . ."

*　　*　　*

For Dakotah, kindergarten was packed with revelations. On the first day the teacher, a fat woman with a pink, hairy sweater, asked each child for a birthday date.

"We'll have a party each time it is somebody's birthday," she said with false excitement. One by one the children named dates, but Dakotah, who had never had or heard of a birthday party, was confused. The boy next to her said, "December nine."

The teacher looked expectantly at Dakotah.

"December nine," she whispered.

"Oh, class! Did you hear that? Dakotah has the same birthday as Billy! That's so wonderful! We'll have a double birthday party! Two children have the same birthday! We'll have two cakes!"

Riding home in the truck with Bonita, Dakotah asked if she had a birthday and if it was December nine.

"Well of course. Everbody has a birthday! Yours is April first, April Fools' Day. That's when you play mean tricks on somebody. Like the April Fool trick your mother pulled on us. Why do you want to know?"

Dakotah explained that the teacher wanted to make many parties at school for birthdays with cakes and games. And she didn't know her birthday. And there was a song.

"Well, we never went in for that birthday stuff. We don't do such foolishness. No wonder the school is always runnin out a money if they spend it on cakes."

She knew she could not tell the teacher her birthday was an April Fool.

In school she learned again what she already knew; that she was different from others, unworthy of friends.

The Listers did their duty, raising Dakotah, Bonita making peanut butter sandwiches for her school lunch while listening to *Morning Glory,* the pre-sunrise program of advertisements, a little news of the sensational kind, prayer and weather reports. The radio voices roared in the bathroom where Verl crouched on the toilet with chronic constipation. His chest pain, which often migrated to some remote interior organ where it pulsed and gnawed, had long baffled the young woman doctor from India who tried to fit into the rural life by uncomprehendingly attending the local amusements of fishing derbies, calcuttas, poker runs and darts tournaments.

"You see Jimmy Mint catch that three-hundred-dollar fish?" she asked to put him at ease. He preferred to describe his torments in exquisite detail, drawing the devious path of a pain with his finger, tracking across his chest, down to his groin, around to the side and back again, rising to the throat.

At last the doctor sent Verl to Salt Lake City for advanced tests. Bonita went with him after arranging for Dakotah to stay with Pastor Alf Crashbee and his wife, Marva.

Dakotah, then seven years old, stood shyly in the hallway while Bonita and Marva Crashbee talked. Mrs. Crashbee spoke in emphatic phrases to set up her salient points. She puffed her cheeks and her nostrils flared. As Dakotah waited to be told where to go and what to do, she fell in love with a candy dish. The single piece of furniture in the hallway was a long, narrow table. On its gleaming surface rested Mrs. Crashbee's car keys. On the farthest end was a small blue plate, close to a saucer in size, and shaped like a fish. On it were seven or eight watermelon-flavored Jolly Rancher candies. It was the amusing shape and color of the dish that entranced, variegated blues ranging from cobalt to flushes of teal. Mrs. Crashbee noticed her gaping and told her to help herself to Jolly Ranchers, thinking that the poor thing probably never had much candy. After Bonita left she said it again in a spasm of urging.

"Go *ahead*! Help your*self*."

Dakotah took one and unwrapped it, not sure where to put the wrapper. The pastor's wife led the way into the kitchen and pointed at a chrome can. When Dakotah tried to lift the lid, the pastor's wife motioned her away, trod on a foot pedal, and the lid flew open. This, too, was novel. She blushed with shame because she had not known about the foot pedal. At her grandparents' house, trash went into a paper grocery bag sitting on a newspaper, and when it was full, the sides grease-stained, the bottom often weakened by wet coffee grounds, it was her job to carry the bag out to the burn barrel. This was the only time she was allowed to light matches, which she did with the gravity of one lighting a vestal hearth, then ran from the stinking smoke.

Bonita came alone to pick her up. She told Mrs. Crashbee that Verl's tests showed serious arthritis in his joints and lumps of bone where old breaks had healed badly, but that not much could be done. He needed a whole new skeleton and his heart was weak. A bull had stepped on his chest when he was twenty and bruised his heart. They told him to take it easy.

"He's at home resting this very minute," said Bonita.

In some way Dakotah's coat sleeve brushed the blue dish off the hall table. Jolly Ranchers skittered along the floor like pale red nuts.

"For pity's sake," said Bonita, bending down to pick up the pieces, "clumsy as a calf." Mrs. Crashbee, shaking her head and thrusting out her chin, said, "It is *noth*ing, just an *old cheap dish,*" but her tone implied it had been part of a set of Royal Worcester. Bonita gave Dakotah a good leg whipping when they got home.

Mrs. Crashbee had a microwave oven that had magically heated the soup for lunch. When Dakotah described this marvel to Bonita a few days later, Verl, who was listening from his chair in the living room, snorted and shouted that he guessed he would

stick with the good old kitchen stove. It was a way of saying there would be no microwave oven for Bonita, who had shown some interest in Dakotah's description.

Thin and with colorless brown-grey hair and greyish eyes, yet with a boy-size nose and chin, no trace of her mother's vivid beauty, in school Dakotah hunched over and kept to herself, considered somewhat stupid by her teachers.

In the fourth grade Sherri Match brought four kittens to school.

"They're for free," she said. "You can choose."

Dakotah instantly wanted the tiny black one with white paws and a diminutive tail that stood straight up. She smoothed him and he purred.

"You can have him," said Sherri grandly, the dispenser of munificence.

Dakotah brought the kitten home under her sweater, where he scratched and wriggled, terribly strong for such a small creature. In Bonita's kitchen she gave him a doll's saucer of milk. He sneezed, then drank greedily. Bonita said nothing, but her expression was chill.

"Where'd that cat come from?" demanded Verl at supper.

"Sherri Match was givin kitties away."

"I bet she was," said Verl grimly. "Well it can't stay here. Cats give me asthma. I'll take it back to them goddamn Matches," and he picked up the kitten and strode out to the truck.

At school the next day Dakotah mumbled to Sherri that she was sorry her granddad had brought the kitten back. "He said cats give him asmar."

Sherri looked at her. "He didn't bring it back. He didn't come to our house. What's asmar?"

*   *   *

As she approached her teens the leg whippings stopped. Bonita seemed to soften through time or remorse. Yet as Dakotah filled out her grandparents became very watchful. She was not allowed to go to anyone's house, or to walk to and from school. Social nights were out, and Bonita told her there would be no dating, as that was the way her mother had been ruined. All around them the gas fields opened up and Verl squinted down the road to see if EnCana or British Petroleum was coming to free him from poverty.

Dakotah was curious about her mother. "Didn't you save any of her stuff?" she asked Bonita after a secret rummage through the attic.

"No, I didn't. I burned those whorish clothes and the stupid pictures she pasted on the walls. She was kind of crazy is what I come to figure. Always makin some mess or doin some outlandish thing. She never did nothin in the kitchen except one time she cooked a whole pot a Minute rice, caught a trout in the stock pond and cut off a piece a that raw trout and laid it on the rice and *ate it. Raw.* I about gagged. That's the kind a thing she did. Crazy stuff."

Dakotah, knowing herself to be unattractive, was too eager to please, hungry beyond measure for affection. She was ready to love anyone. Sash Hicks, a skinny boy dressed perpetually in camouflage clothing, with a face and body that seemed to have been broken and then realigned, noticed her, attracted to her shy silence. She responded with long, intense stares when she

thought he wasn't looking and daydreams that never went farther than swooning kisses. One day Mr. Lewksberry, the history teacher, in an effort to make his despised subject more interesting, pandered to the local definition of history by assigning his students an essay on western outlaws. In the school library, turning the pages of the *Encyclopedia of Western Badmen,* Dakotah came on a photograph of Billy the Kid. It seemed Sash Hicks was looking up from the page, the same smirky triumph in the face, the slouched posture and dirty pants. Sash immediately gained a lustrous aura of outlawry and gun expertise. Now in her daydreams they rode away together, Sash twisting back in the saddle to shoot at their pursuers, Verl and Bonita. In real life Dakotah and Sash began to think of themselves as a couple, meeting in hallways, sitting near each other in classes, exchanging notes. She felt he was her only chance to get away from Bonita and Verl, that the distance between them could be bridged by grappling. She loved him. At home she kept Sash a secret.

In the beginning of their senior year Sash Hicks made up his mind. No judge of character, he gauged her a biddable handmaiden who would look to his comforts. He said, Let's get married, and she agreed. She expected her grandparents would boil with rage when they heard the news. She said it quickly at the dinner table. They were pleased. She had not realized that they shared her feeling of unjust imprisonment from their own perspective.

"You'll get along good with Sash," said Verl, jovial with relief that she would soon be off his hands.

"Too bad Shaina didn't think a that, might a saved her," mumbled Bonita, who never gave up on the subject. Their approval was the closest to praise they had ever bestowed on her.

Dakotah dropped out of school a few months before graduation. The school counselor, Mrs. Lenski, middle-aged and with murky blue eyes outlined in brown, tried to persuade her to fin-ish. "Oh, I know how you feel, I completely understand that you want to get married, but believe me, you will *never never* regret finishing school. If you should have to get a job or if trouble comes—"

No, thought Dakotah, you don't know how I feel, you don't know what it is like to be me, but she said nothing. She found a waitressing job at Big Bob's travel stop. The pay was minimum wage and the tips rarely more than dimes or quarters but enough for them to rent a three-room apartment over the Elks lodge.

Otto and Virginia Hicks and Verl and Bonita came with them to the town clerk's office on Dakotah's day off. After the brief cer-emony, aware that some kind of celebration was proper, they went to Big Bob's and sat in a booth, surrounded by truckers and gas field workers. Mr. Castle, the manager, gave them free drinks and his best wishes. Sash picked at a sore on his upper lip and ate three Big Bobbers with a quart-size milk shake. Dakotah ordered hot chocolate with whipped cream. Mrs. Hicks spilled cola on her lilac skirt and became impatient to get home and sponge it off.

"I hope it don't stain," she mourned.

The Hickses were famous for their card parties at which canasta was the game of choice and the first prize was one of Vir-ginia Hicks's pecan pies, for she came from Texas and prided her-self on them. Otto Hicks had met her when, as a young man just out of college, he went to Amarillo for a job interview with a drill-bit manufacturer. He wore his cowboy hat and boots and barn jacket and did not get the job. Yet he persuaded Virginia, their head receptionist, to walk out without notice and come with him to Wyoming, and that was some satisfaction. As an added revenge, when he walked past the personnel manager's parking space he had scratched the door of the man's car with a hoof pick that he had in his pocket. Back in Wyoming, Otto got into the snow fence business, subcontracting for the state highway department.

Bonita and Verl, leaving their balled-up greasy napkins on the table instead of putting them in the disposal bin, also hurried away as Verl felt his old pain encroaching, moving stealthily toward his heart. None of them knew what it was like having a serious medical condition, Verl thought, or what it was like waking in the morning and never knowing if he would see the yard light come on at twilight. He had given up on the clinic doctors and now followed the local practice of consulting a chiropractor, the most favored Jacky Barstow, a fat man with steel rod fingers. The chiropractor told him his problem was in his spine, and most ailments, including cancer, were caused by bad, jammed-up spines. Verl's spine, he said, was one of the worst he had ever seen. Verl slid out of the booth and Bonita followed. Dakotah, unable to shake off her job training, picked up after them, threw the cups and paper wrappers in the trash bin, something Sash Hicks (and Mr. Castle) noticed with approval. No one had paid for the food, and Mr. Castle told Dakotah he would deduct the cost from her next paycheck.

Sash Hicks was not the first naked man Dakotah had seen. When she was fourteen Bonita fell down the porch steps because of her arthritic knee's stiffness and pain and broke her left arm. The new doctor at the clinic, a slab-sided fiftyish woman, after talking on the phone with Bonita's regular doctor, who was treating her for the arthritis, ignored her furious glare and said it was the ideal time to get that recommended knee replacement as she would be laid up for weeks anyway.

"You're not getting any younger, Bonita," she said, showing her the X-rays. "The right knee looks pretty good, but the bones are very worn and diseased in the left. It can't get better by itself, especially if you persist in ignoring the situation. The replacement will let you get around pretty well. You'll have years of painless movement." Bonita protested, but Verl said she should go ahead with it, and after her arm was set they moved her to a hospital room for knee surgery.

Verl came home from the hospital around noon carrying bags of groceries and several bottles of whiskey. He said that Bonita would be back home in ten days encased in two casts.

"So you'll have to pretty much take care a the kitchen."

He seemed a little excited, putting steaks in a Pyrex dish and shaking Tabasco and Texas barbecue sauce onto them, sprinkling coarse salt and pepper. He made a long, rectangular fire on the ground, cowboy style, saying it would burn down to a good bed of coals. He told Dakotah to get some potatoes ready for baking. Dakotah caught some of his excitement; it was a vacation from Bonita and her rules, a kind of picnic for her and Verl. But around four o'clock the real reason for the steaks showed up—Harlan, Verl's brother who worked for the Bureau of Land Management in Crack Springs. Harlan was short and muscular and very quiet. His hair was longer than Verl's. He wore brown plastic-framed glasses. Whenever he visited conversation died away and they all stared at the curtains or picked at their cuticles until someone, usually Bonita, said, "Well, I got to get somethin done," rose and left the room. But now, without Bonita, a kind of conversation sprang up between the two brothers, a discussion of an old schoolmate who had been indicted for embezzling the town's Arbor Day tree fund. While the fire sank into shimmering coals they sat on the ground and drank the whiskey, then Verl laid the two steaks directly on the coals. Clouds of fragrant smoke spread out and after a minute he stabbed the meat with a long-handled fork and turned it over. Black coals and ash stuck to the charred steaks. Harlan held out a tin pie pan and Verl got the meat onto it. They went into the kitchen. Neither of them said anything to Dakotah until she put the baked potatoes on the table with the butter dish. She had figured out that the steaks were only for the men.

"Still hard in the middle, dammit," said Verl. "Don't you know how to bake a potato?" But they ate them and then, ignoring her, went into the living room to watch television crime shows and drink more whiskey. She made herself the old reliable peanut butter sandwich.

During the night some unfamiliar sound like an Indian whoop woke her, but she heard nothing more. She got up to go to the bathroom, tiptoeing in the dark past the guest room where Harlan would be sleeping. But the door was open and the moonlight shone on an undisturbed bed. Maybe, she thought, after all that whiskey he was sleeping on the couch. She turned the corner toward the bathroom, switched on the hall light as the door to Bonita and Verl's bedroom opened. Harlan came out. He was naked, his eyes dazed. His sexual parts looked large and dark. He seemed not to see Dakotah and she fled back to her room and down the back stairs, going into the yard rather than risk the path to the bathroom again.

Sash Hicks discovered her quiet demeanor masked gritty stubbornness. After a few weeks, when they weren't rolling on the new Super-Puff mattress, they were fighting over issues petty and large.

"Chrissake," said Hicks, who was still in school working toward his goal of becoming a computer programmer, "all I asked was for you to get me a beer and some a them chips and the salsa. That goin a break your arm?"

"Get it yourself. I been bossed around since I was a kid. I didn't agree to be your maid. I worked a full shift and I'm tired. You should be gettin *me* a beer. You act like a customer. Go on, talk to the manager and get me fired!" She surprised herself. Where had this hard attitude come from? It was something in her, and it must be from her rebellious, unknown mother. And maybe also from Bonita, who had her own raspy side when Verl wasn't around.

Hicks, aggrieved at her stubbornness, saw he had made a dreadful mistake. Plus she was flat-chested. After months of her obstinate refusals to bring him tools or beers or to pull off his stinking sneakers, they had it out. He said he was through and she said good, but she was keeping the apartment since she paid the rent. In a flare of accusations and blames they agreed to divorce. He moved back to his parents' house and indulged in a debauch of drinking and partying to celebrate his new freedom. When he failed his final exams, he joined the army, telling his father that the army would train him in computer programming and he'd get paid for it, too. It was even better than his original plan—it really would let him be all he could be. He used the enlistment bonus for a down payment on a new truck which his family would keep for him until he came back.

But before he left for basic training, Dakotah discovered she was pregnant.

"Oh my god," said Bonita. "You get hold a Sash Hicks right now."

"What for? We are gettin a divorce. He's goin in the army. Me and Sash are through."

"Not if you are havin his baby. You're not through by a long shot. You better call him up right now and stop this divorce mess."

But Dakotah would not call him. Why, she wanted to ask Bonita, didn't you and Verl stop me from marrying him? But she knew that if they had protested she would have run off with Sash to spite them.

The months went by. Dakotah kept working at Big Bob's, enjoying the apartment, having all that room to herself. Sometimes she talked to the absent Sash Hicks. "Get me a glass a champagne, Sash. And a turkey sandwich. With mayo and pickles. Run down the store and pick up some chocolate puddin. What's the matter, cat got your tongue?" She planned to keep the apartment after the baby came. She had not considered who would take care of the baby while she worked.

One day Mrs. Lenski, the school counselor, came into Big Bob's and sat in a booth by herself. She pulled a tissue from her purse and blew her nose, sopped at her watery eyes.

"Why Dakotah. I wondered where you were these days. I see you and Sash are expecting. Excuse me, I think I'm getting the flu."

"I'm expecting. He don't even know. We broke up. You were right. It would of been better if I graduated. Get a better job than *this.*" She gestured at the booths, at the cubbyhole where the orders from the kitchen came out, Adam and Eve on a raft, axle grease, Mike and Ike, and Big Bob's super burger, called a "bomb" in the kitchen.

"It could be worse," said Mrs. Lenski. "You could have been a school counselor. Heartbreaker job." She gave Dakotah her card and said they would stay in touch. She came in once a week after that and always asked what Dakotah was doing, planning, thinking of for the future, those questions that adults believed occupied the thoughts of the young. Dakotah had no plans for the future; the present seemed solid.

Mr. Castle asked her to come into his office, a windowless hole that barely contained his desk. A huge tinted photograph of his wife and triplet daughters took up most of the desktop. Boxes of paper cups were piled up in the corner. Mr. Castle had a red, jolly face and a store of mossy jokes. He got along with everyone, calmed difficult customers as a snake charmer soothes irritable cobras.

"Well, Dakotah," he began. "I don't have no problem with you havin a baby, but the company got a policy that no lady more than six months gone can work here."

"That's not fair," said Dakotah. "I need this job. Sash and me split up. I'm on my own. I work hard for you, Mr. Castle."

"Oh, I know that, Dakotah, but it's not for me to say." He cast a husband's practiced eye over her. "That baby is expected pretty damn soon, right? Like in a few weeks? You can't fool me, Dakotah, so don't try." All the jolliness had dried up. She understood she was being fired.

The boy was born six days later, and Mr. Castle winced as he realized how close they had come to having a delivery during noon rush hour. He sent a potted chrysanthemum with a card saying, "From the Gang at Big Bob's!"

Dakotah had somehow expected the baby to be a quiet creature she would care for as one cared for a pet. She was unprepared for the child's roaring greediness, his assertion of self, or for the violence of love that swamped her, that made her shake with what she knew must come next.

"I guess I got a put the baby up for adoption," she said to Bonita, then broke down and bawled. "I had money saved up for

the doctor, but now I don't have my job and can't pay the rent."
Bonita was aghast. The boy was legitimate, though deserted by
his father. She could almost hear the Matches sneering that
Bonita and Verl would not care for their own flesh and blood.
And he was a boy!

"You can't bring more shame on this family. It's almost as bad
as what your mother done. You come up with some support
money from that no-good bum you married and your granddad
and me will take care a the child. We'll have to do it. Your
mother's sin unto the second generation. I want you to call up
Mrs. Hicks and tell her that her precious son skipped out on his
child. Tell her that you are goin to the child support people and a
lawyer. I'll bet you anything he give the enlistment bonus to his
folks."

Dakotah did telephone Mrs. Hicks and asked for Sash's
address.

"I spose you want a squeeze money out a him," said Mrs.
Hicks. "He is in the army and we don't know where. Someplace
in California. He didn't tell us where they was sendin him. Probably Eye-rack by now. He said he was bein deployed to Eye-rack.
But we don't know for sure. He didn't tell *me*." There was bitterness in her voice, perhaps the bitterness of the neglected mother
or of someone wishing to be in the land of fresh pecans.

Bonita sighed. "She's lyin. She knows where he is. But them
Hickses stick together tighter than cuckleburrs. We'll have to
take care a him. You name that baby Verl after your granddad.
That'll make him more interested to help the boy." She sighed.
"Does it ever end?" she asked and in her mind phrased a prayer-
ful request for strength.

Among the privileges of western malehood from which the
baby benefited were opened dams of affection in Bonita and
Verl. Dakotah was amazed at the way Verl hung over the infant's

crib mouthing nonsense words, but she understood what had happened. It was the same knife slice of lightning love that had cut her. He wanted Dakotah to change the child's last name to Lister, but she said that although Sash Hicks was a rat, he was still the legal and legitimate father and the baby would stay a Hicks.

Nor could Sash Hicks be located. He had been at Fort Irwin National Training Center and had sent home a cryptic letter. "I learned some Arab words. Na'am. Marhaba. Marhaba means hello. Na'am means yes. So you know."

Neither Bonita nor Verl would hear of Dakotah going on welfare or accepting social services, for the Matches would rightly condemn them as weak-kneed sucks on the taxpayer's tit. They talked it through at night, the yard light casting its corrosive glare on the south wall. She could go back to Mr. Castle and beg for her old job. Bonita and Vern would care for the baby. Or—

"Way we see it," said Bonita to Dakotah, "is *you* ought a join the army yourself. They take women. You can support Little Verl that way. Finish your education. And find out how to get through the red tape that will track down Sash Hicks. Me and Big Verl will take care a him until you get through with the army. A job at Big Bob's don't pay enough."

Verl added his opinion. "When you come back you can get a real good job. And if you can get one a them digital cameras cheap at the PX, we'll take pictures a him—" He nodded at the baby sleeping in his carry chair.

She could not believe how solicitous they had become. It was as though their icy hearts had melted and the leg whippings had never happened, as though they were bound by consanguineous affection instead of grudging duty in obeisance to community mores. She marveled that this change of heart was rooted in involuntary love, a love that had not moved them when they brought her as an infant to the ranch.

Her grandfather himself drove her to the recruitment office in Crack Springs, harping all the way on duty, responsibility, the necessity for signing the papers so child support could come to them. He also drove her to the Military Entrance Processing Station in Cody. He had even picked out a specialty for her: combat medic.

"I checked around," he said, winking his pinpoint aquamarine eyes, which, as he aged, had almost disappeared under colorless eyebrows and hanging folds of flesh. "EMTs make good money. You could get to be a medic and when you come back, why there's your career, just waiting." The word "career" sounded strange coming out of his mouth. For years he had ranted against wives who worked out of the home. On the ranches the wives held everything together cooking for big crowds, nursing the sick and injured, cleaning, raising children and driving them to rodeo practice, keeping the books and paying the bills, making mail runs and picking up feed at the farm supply, taking the dogs in for their shots, and often riding with the men at branding and shipping times, and in mountainous country helping with the annual shove up and shove down shifting cattle to and from pasturage leased from the Forest Service, and were treated with little more regard than the beef they helped produce.

It was almost spring, last night's small snow spiking up the dead grass in ragged points, balling in the yellow joints of the stream-side willow, snow that would melt as soon as the sun touched it. She was joining the army, leaving behind the seedy two-story town, the dun-colored prairie flattened by wind, leaving the gumbo roads, the radio voices flailing through nets of static, the gossip and narrow opinions. As they drove through the town, she saw the muddy truck that was always parked in front of the bar, the kid named Bub Carl who hung around the barbershop. The sun was up, warming the asphalt, and already heat waves ran across the road as the old landscape fell away behind her. Yet she felt nothing for the place or herself, not even relief at escaping Verl and Bonita, or sorrow or regret at putting the baby in their care. As for the child, she would be coming back to him. He would wait, as she had waited, but for him there would be a happy ending, for she would return. She picked him up and stared into his slate blue eyes.

"See? I'm comin back to get you. I'm coming back for you. I love you and will come back. Promise." She just had to get through the dense period of life away from the ranch, away from Wyoming, away from her baby who gave the place its only value.

She went to Fort Leonard Wood in Missouri for basic training. The first thing she learned was that it was still a man's army and that women were decidedly inferior in all ways. The memory flashed of a time when she had gone shopping with Bonita in Cody. Bonita favored a pint-size mall that featured Cowboy Meats, Radio Shack and a video store. Dakotah chose to wait in the truck instead of trailing after Bonita, who was a ruthless and vociferous shopper for the cheapest of everything. Dakotah watched a man and his two children outside Grum's Dollar Mart, where there was a tiny patch of grass. The man had a hard red face and brown mustache. He was dressed in jeans, dirty undershirt and ball cap, but wore ranch work boots. He was throwing a Frisbee gently to the boy, a slow toddler unable to catch it. Against the Dollar Mart wall stood the girl, a year or two older than the boy, but the father did not throw the Frisbee to her. Dakotah hated the way he ignored the girl's yearning gaze. She smiled at the girl staring so fixedly at the father and son. At last Dakotah got out of the truck and walked over.

"Hey there," she said to the girl, smiling. "What's your name?"

The child did not answer but flattened herself against the grimy wall.

"What d'*you* want?" said the father, letting his arm down, the Frisbee sagging against his leg. It was a nylon Frisbee, the kind dog owners favored.

The toddler was yelling at the father. "Frow! Frow!" When the man did not throw the Frisbee, the boy began to whine and blub.

"Nothin. Just sayin hello. To the little girl."

"Yeah. Well, here comes your granny. Git home and don't be botherin my kids." The little girl gave her a look of pure hatred and stuck out a long, yellow tongue.

Bonita wedged the bags of groceries between two bags of garbage she intended to drop off at the landfill. "What're you doin talkin a him?"

"I wasn't! I was sayin hello to the little girl. Who are they?"

"He's Rick Sminger, one a Shaina's old . . . friends. Least said about him the better. I was you I wouldn't ask no questions. Get in and let's get goin."

The worst thing about the army, the thing she knew she could never get used to, was the constant presence of too many people, too close, in her face, radiating heat and smells, talking and shouting. Someone who has grown up in silence and vast space, who was born to solitude, who feels different and shrinks from notice, suffers in the company of others. So homesickness took the shape of longing for wind, an empty landscape, for silence and privacy. She longed for the baby and came to believe she was homesick for the old ranch.

She made a low score on the aptitude test, edging into the borderline just enough to continue on. She thought about Verl's suggestion she become a combat medic. She had no other ideas. At least she would be helping people. She named it as her choice of a Military Occupational Specialty. During basic training she heard that becoming a combat medic was very tough. Candidates went crazy, they said, because of the enormous amounts of information they had to memorize. But she had learned CPR in sophomore gym class and thought she could study enough to pass a few tests.

After basic training she went to Fort Sam Houston in San Antonio for EMT training, and the immediate future loomed like a cliff. All of her fellow volunteers seemed to have been practicing medicine since kindergarten. Pat Moody, a wiry blonde from Oregon, was the daughter of a doctor and had heard medical talk for years. She was excited about training at Brooks Medical Center because of its famous burn unit and planned to become a doctor after she got out of the army. Marnie Jellson came from a potato farm in Idaho and had cared for her sick mother for two years. When the mother died she had enlisted. Tommet Means had been an EMT since high school. Chris Jinkla came from a family of veterinarians and had accompanied his father on calls a thousand times.

"I grew up bandaging paws," he said.

She and Pat and Marnie became friends. Pat played the guitar and taught Dakotah enough chords to string together "Michael, Row the Boat Ashore." Marnie had a collection of movies that they watched on weekends. Marnie had a potato tattooed on her left calf and knew dozens of potato jokes. Both of them talked about their families, and finally Dakotah explained that her grandparents had bought her up, told about Sash and the breakup and the baby.

"You poor kiddo," said Marnie. "You've been through a lot."

"How can it be," Dakotah asked them, "that you feel homesick for a place you hate?" She thought of the neutral smell of dust like stones or old wood, of summer haze from distant forest fires, of rose-rock outcrops breaking from the rusty earth. She thought of the run-down town, every other building sporting a weathered For Sale sign.

"Maybe it's the people you are homesick for, not the place," said Pat.

And of course it was. She saw that right away. Not just Baby Verl, but even closed-up Bonita and Verl hitching along on his bad legs.

She bought a camera and sent it to Bonita and Verl, begging them to take photographs of Baby Verl. She taped the dozens of them on her wall. She wrote long letters to the baby, covered the margins with symbols of kisses and hugs. She and Pat and Marnie raided the PX for baby toys, miniature blue jeans, pajamas imprinted with tanks and planes.

They went to dinner at restaurants and Dakotah learned it was bad manners to stack the empty dishes. "I was just helpin the waitress out," she explained. It was what ranch people did after finishing their burgers at Big Bob's.

At a Japanese place one night Pat persuaded her to try sushi.

"What is it?" she asked, looking at the hump of rice with an orange slice of something on top.

"It is salmon and rice, and that is wasabi, a kind of grated horseradish. It's hot."

She ate it, and the texture of the salmon startled her. "It's not cooked!"

"It's not supposed to be cooked."

"It's raw! Raw fish! I ate it." Her stomach heaved but she kept it down and even ate another. A day later she remembered Bonita describing Shaina putting raw trout on some Minute rice. Was it possible that her mother had heard somewhere about sushi and decided to try it—Wyoming style? Was it possible her mother had been exhibiting not craziness but curiosity about the outside world? She told Pat and Marnie about it and they decided that was it—curiosity and longing for the exotic.

As the tsunami of reading material, lectures, slides, videos, X-rays, computer tutorials on anatomy, diseases, trauma, physiology, obstetrics, pediatrics, shock and a bewildering vocabulary of medical terms swept over the group, Dakotah did not think she would pass the EMT Basic Registry Exam. And even if she did, then came primary care training and the horror courses in chemical, explosive and radiation injuries.

"I will never get to Whiskey level," she said calmly to Pat, thinking of needle chest compression and clearing airways, both of which she dreaded.

"Come on. You'll make it," said Pat, who aced every test. "Those are situational exercises, which makes it real interesting." Dakotah passed the EMT test, but at the bottom of the class. Marnie flat-out failed.

"Suggest you think about changin to military police," said the squinty-eyed, spotted-banana-skin instructor to Dakotah. "Medicine is not your thing. I know I'd sure hate to be lyin there with my guts hangin out and here comes old rough-hand Dakotah tryin to remember what to do."

Pat went to Fort Drum in New York for training at the medical simulation center, where darkness, explosions and smoke mimicked realistic battlefield situations. She sent Marnie and Dakotah a letter describing Private Hunk, a computerized patient-simulation mannequin who could bleed, breathe, even talk a little. He was complete in the last detail, constructed for countless intubations, tracheotomies, catheterizations. He suffered sucking chest wounds, hideous traumas. He bled and moaned for help and on occasion shrieked an inhuman birdcall like a falcon. He was hot or cold, at the instructor's wish, could run a fever or suffer severe hypothermia.

"He's got a cute little dick. I'm in love with him," wrote Pat. Dakotah answered the letter, but they never heard from Pat again.

There were many letters from Bonita, the words looping downhill across the page and ending with a two-line prayer. She always began the letter with news of Baby Verl's progress with cutting teeth, crawling, standing up, how Verl's old dog Bum had taken to him, following him everywhere and letting Baby pull his ears, how Verl had got another dog, Buddy, because Bum was getting old, and how Buddy loved the baby even more than Bum, and only when she had detailed every wonderful thing Baby Verl had done did she report on local events. Her sister Juanita had come from Casper for a visit and to show off her new husband, who worked in the gas fields for Triangle Energy. The first husband, Don, had worked for the same company. He had believed fall-protection gear was for pantywaists and died when he reached for a hoist-lifted pipe and missed. Big Verl, Bonita wrote, had quit his chiropractor and was now going to a fat woman who gave massages and charged terrific prices. "At least she advertises they are massages. If Verl wasn't Verl I would think it was something else." Dakotah felt a rare and even painful rush of affection mixed with pity for Bonita, although she suspected she was only writing out of a sense of duty.

A few letters came from Mrs. Lenski, alternately sardonic and cheerful. It seemed to Dakotah that as soon as she had left, the town started dying off. One of the Vasey twins had been killed and the other severely injured in a car crash at the intersection where everybody knew to slow down. Some truck with Colorado plates had blasted through and T-boned them. And, wrote Mrs. Lenski, two lesbian women with a herd of goats had bought the Tin Can house and planned to make cheese and sell it locally. Dakotah was shocked to see the word "lesbian" on the page of a letter like any ordinary word. Tug Diceheart and two other hands riding for the Tic-Tac had been caught making meth in the bunkhouse and arrested. Juiciest of all, Mrs. Match had left Wyatt and returned to California to become a real estate agent. Dakotah wondered if Verl was gloating.

Both Dakotah and Marnie changed their MOS to Military Police. They had become closest friends, closer than she had ever been to Sash. Dakotah, for the first time in her life, had someone to talk to, someone who understood everything, from rural ways to failing at tests. Marnie said maybe they were in love. They talked about setting up house together with Baby Verl after they got out. One day they were in a Humvee, Dakotah clutching a machine gun, on their way to a checkpoint to search Iraqi women.

"Yup, here we are with the fuckups. MP is where the dumb ones end up. Supposed a be the stupidest part of the entire army."

"Don't you think some of the officers could get that prize?"

"Yeah. So probably MPs come second. Second dumbest, something to brag about."

They had learned that the checkpoints were intensely danger-ous, and after a few weeks Dakotah developed a little magic ritual to keep herself alive. She rapidly twitched the muscles of her toes, heel, calf, knee, hip, waist, shoulder, eyebrow, elbow, wrist, thumb, fingers on the right side and then repeated the series for the left side. Bonita had sent her a silver-plated cross that she recognized. It had always been in the second drawer of the kitchen dresser with a tortoiseshell comb, a pot holder too nice to use, a pair of small kid gloves that had belonged to Verl's famous great-grandmother, a red box with a sliding lid filled with old buttons. She wore the cross once, but it tangled with her dog tags and she put it away.

She hated searching the Iraqi women, knew that they hated her doing it. Some of them smelled, and their voluminous, often ragged and dusty burkas could conceal everything from a black market radio to baby clothes to a bomb. One young woman had six glossy eggplants hidden under her garment. Dakotah pitied her, unable even to buy and carry home a few eggplants without an American soldier groping at her. Never had the world seemed so vile and her own problems so mean and petty.

On the day the IED exploded under the Humvee she had not completed the left side of the protecting muscle twitches, choosing a third cup of coffee instead. It happened too suddenly for anything to register. One moment they were traveling fast, the next she was looking up into the face of Chris Jinkla.

"Moooo," she said, trying to make a cow joke for the veterinary's son, but he didn't recognize her and thought she was moaning. She felt nothing at that moment and tried her magic muscle twitch sequence, but something was wrong on the right side.

"I'm fine, Chris. Except my arm."

The medic was startled. He peered into her bloody face. "My god, it's Pat, right?"

"Dakotah," she whispered. "I'm Dakotah. I'm fine but I need my arm. Please look for it. I can't go home without it." She turned her head and saw a heap of bloody rags and a patch of skin.

"Marnie?"

Her right arm was still there though cruelly shattered, and the best they could hope for, said the doctor at the field hospital, was to amputate and save enough stump to carry a prosthetic. "You're young and strong," he said. "You'll make it."

"I'm fine," she agreed. "How about Marnie?" She knew as she asked.

The doctor gave her a look.

She was shipped out to Germany with other wounded, gradually aware that there was some awful knowledge hovering, something worse than her mangled arm, which had been amputated, something as bad as losing Marnie. Maybe they had discovered she had cancer and wouldn't tell her. But it was not until she was sent to Walter Reed that she heard the bad news from Bonita herself, who stood at her bedside with a curious expression of mingled sorrow and, looking at the stump of her arm, a ghoulish curiosity.

"Oh, oh," she whispered, and then burst into streaming tears. Never had Dakotah seen anyone cry that way, tears pouring down Bonita's cheeks to the corners of her mouth, splashing from her jawline onto her rayon blouse as though her head was filled with water. She could not speak for long minutes.

"Baby Verl," she finally said.

"*What?*" Dakotah knew instinctively it was the worst thing.

"Ridin in the back a Big Verl's truck—" And the tears began again. "He fell out."

The story came slowly and wetly. The eighteen-month-old child had loved riding with his great-grandfather, but this day Verl put him with the dogs in the open truck bed. Big Verl was so proud to have a boy and wanted him to be tough. The dogs loved him. She said that several times. The rest of it came in a rush.

"See, Verl thought he'd just sit with the dogs. They done it

214

before. But you know how dogs hang over the edge. Baby Verl did that too, near as we can tell, so that when the truck went down in one a them dips it threw him out. It was a accident. He fell under the wheels, Dakotah. Big Verl is half-crazy. They got him sedated. The doctors are fixin it up for you to come home."

Dakotah threw back her head and howled. She snapped her teeth at Bonita and began to curse her and Verl. How could he be so stupid as to put a baby in the bed of a pickup? The shouting and crying brought an irritated nurse, who asked them to keep it down. Bonita, who had been backing away, turned and ran into the corridor and did not come back.

"It takes a year, Dakotah," said Mrs. Parka, the grief counselor, a full-bosomed woman with enormous liquid eyes. "A full turn of the seasons before you begin to heal. Time *does* heal all wounds, and right now the passage of time is the best medicine. And you yourself must heal physically as well as spiritually. You need to be very strong. What is your religion?"

Dakotah shook her head. She had asked the woman to write to Mrs. Lenski for her and tell her what happened, but the woman said it was part of the healing process for Dakotah to face the fact of Baby Verl's passing and tell Mrs. Lenski herself. Dakotah wanted to choke the woman until she went blue-black and died.

She glared furiously.

"There are other ways for you to communicate. The telephone. E-mail?"

"Get away from me," said Dakotah.

At the end of the summer she was still there, in a grimy old motel somehow connected to the hospital, getting used to the prosthesis. She sat in the dim room doing nothing. Dreary days went by. She struggled to understand the morass of papers about disability allowances, death allowances, Baby Verl's support. One of the official letters said that support payments for baby Verl Hicks should never have been paid for, by or through Dakotah, but through the child's father, SSgt Saskatoon M. Hicks, currently at Walter Reed Hospital recuperating.

That Sash was somewhere at the same hospital amazed her. That she had learned about it amazed her more, for the legendary confusion and chaos of lost patients was like the nest of rattlesnakes Verl had once showed her, a coiling, twisting mass under a shelving boulder. He had fired his old 12-gauge at them and still the torn flesh twisted.

One afternoon a volunteer, Mrs. Glossbeau, came to her. Dakotah saw she must be rich; she was trim and tanned and wore an elegant raspberry-colored wool suit with a white silk shirt.

"Are you Dakotah Hicks?"

She had forgotten they were still married. Sash's divorce action had gone dormant when he left for basic training.

"Yes, but we were gettin a divorce. And then I don't know what happened."

"Well, your husband is here in the complex and his doctors think you ought to see him. I should warn you, he has suffered very severe injuries. He may not recognize you. He probably won't. They are hoping that seeing you again will . . . sort of wake him up."

Dakotah said nothing at first. She did not want to see Sash. She wanted to see Marnie. She wanted Baby Verl. She half-believed he was waiting to play patty-cake. She could feel his small warm hands.

"I don't really want to see him. We got nothin to talk about."

But the woman sat beside her chair and cajoled. Dakotah breathed in a delicious fragrance, as rich as apricots in cream and with the slight bitterness from the cyanide kernel. The woman's hands were shapely with long pale nails, her fingers laden with diamond-heavy rings. Because it seemed the only way to get rid of the woman was to agree, in the end she went.

Sash Hicks had disintegrated, both legs blown off at midthigh, the left side of his face a mass of shiny scar tissue, the left ear and eye gone. It was almost like seeing Marnie, whom she knew was dead, although she kept on hearing her voice in corridors. Sash's nurse told her that he had suffered brain damage. But Dakotah recognized him, old Billy the Kid shot up by Pat Garrett. More than ever he looked like the antique outlaw. He stared at the ceiling with his right eye. The ruined face showed no comprehension except that something was terribly wrong if he could only know what.

"Sash. It's me, Dakotah."

He said nothing. Although his face was ruined and he was ravaged from the waist down, his right shoulder and arm were muscular and stout.

She didn't know what she felt for him—pity or nothing at all.

Words came out of the distorted mouth.

"Ah—ah—eh." He subsided as though someone had unscrewed the valve that kept his body inflated and upright. His moment of grappling with the world had passed and his chin sank onto his chest.

"Are you asleep?" asked Dakotah. There was no answer and she left.

*   *   *

The trip to the ranch was hard, but there was nowhere else to go. She dreaded seeing Verl; would she scream and punch him? Grab the .30-.30 on top of the dish cupboard and shoot him? She felt a scorching rage and at the same time was listless and inert, slumping on the backseat of the taxi. Sonny Ezell's old vehicle moved very slowly. Her prosthesis was in her suitcase. She knew they had to see the arm stump to believe, just as she had to see little Verl's grave.

They passed the Match ranch, unchanged, and turned onto Sixteen Mile. The days were shortening, but there was still plenty of light, the top of Table Butte, layered bands of buff, gamboge and violet, gilded by the setting sun. The shallow river, as yellow as lemon rind, lay flaccid between denuded banks. The dying sun hit the willows, transforming them into bloody wands. Light reflected from the road as from glass. They seemed to be traveling through a hammered red landscape in which ranch buildings appeared dark and sorrowful. She knew what blood-soaked ground was, knew that severed arteries squirted like the backyard hose. A dog came out of the ditch and ran into a stubble field. They passed the Persa ranch, where the youngest son had drowned in last spring's flood. She realized that every ranch she passed had lost a boy, lost them early and late, boys smiling, sure in their risks, healthy, tipped out of the current of life by liquor and acceleration, rodeo smashups, bad horses, deep irrigation ditches, high trestles, tractor rollovers and "unloaded" guns. Her boy, too. This was the waiting darkness that surrounded ranch boys, the dangerous growing up that canceled their favored status. The trip along this road was a roll call of grief. Wind began to lift the fine dust and the sun set in haze.

When she got out at the house the wind swallowed her whole, snatching at her scarf, huffing up under the hem of her coat, eeling up her sleeve. She could feel the grit. Every step she took dried weeds snapped under her shoes. Sonny Ezell carried her suitcase to the porch and wouldn't take any money. Someone inside switched on the porch light.

She did not attack Verl. Both of her grandparents hugged her and cried. Verl thudded to his knees and sobbed that he was sorry unto death. He pressed his wet face against her hand. He had never before touched her in any way. She felt nothing and took it to mean recovery. There was a large color photograph of little Verl on the wall. He was sitting on a bench with one chubby leg folded under, the other dangling and showing a snowy white stocking and miniature sneaker. He held a plush bear by its ear. They must have taken him to the Wal-Mart portrait studio. They had sent her a print of the same picture.

Bonita brought out a big dinner, fried chicken, mashed potatoes, string beans with cream sauce, fresh rolls and for dessert a pecan pie that she said Mrs. Hicks had sent over. She said something about Mrs. Hicks that Dakotah did not catch. It was a terrible dinner. None of them could eat. They pushed the food around and in hoarse teary voices said how good everything looked. Verl, perhaps trying to set an example, took a forkful of mashed potato and retched. At last they got up. Bonita wrapped the food with plastic film and put it in the refrigerator.

"We'll eat it tomorrow," she said.

They sat in awful silence in the living room, the television set dark.

"Your old room is made up," said Bonita. In the quiet the kitchen refrigerator hummed like wind in the wires. "You know, them Hickses couldn't afford to go to Warshinton and see Sash. They need to know about him. They can't find out a thing. They telephoned a hunderd times. Every time they call that hospital they get cut off or transferred to somebody don't know. They need for you to tell them. It's bad, them not knowing."

She could not tell them how much worse it was to know.

The next morning was somewhat easier; they could all drink hot coffee. Mourning, grief and loss were somehow eased by hot, black coffee. But still no one could eat. At noon Dakotah left Verl and Bonita and went for a walk up the pine slope. A new power line ran through the slashed trees.

At supper the welcome-home meal reappeared, heated in Bonita's microwave that she had bought with some of Dakotah's money. They finally ate, very slowly. In a low voice Dakotah said that the chicken was good. It had no taste. Bonita made more coffee—none of them would sleep anyway—and cut Mrs. Hicks's pecan pie. Verl gazed at the golden triangle on his saucer, seemed unable to lift his fork.

There was the creak of the kitchen door and Otto and Virginia Hicks came in, tentatively. Bonita urged them to sit down, got coffee for them. Mrs. Hicks's red eyes went to Dakotah. The older woman's hand shook and the coffee cup stuttered against the saucer. She suddenly gave up on the coffee and pushed it away.

"What about Sash?" she blurted. "You seen him. We got that official letter that says he is coming home. They don't say how bad he was hurt. We can't find out nothing. He don't call us. Maybe he can't call us. What about Sash?"

Bonita looked at Dakotah, opened her mouth to say something, then closed it again.

The silence spread out like a rain-swollen river, lapping against the walls of the room, mounting over their heads. Dakotah thought of Ezell's taxi rolling slowly past the bereft ranches. She felt the Hickses' fear begin to solidify into knowledge. Already grief was settling around the tense couple like a rope loop, the same rope that encircled all of them. She had to draw the Hickses' rope tight and snub them up to the pain until they went numb, show that it didn't pay to love.

"Sash," she said at last so softly they could barely hear. "Sash is tits-up in a ditch."

They sat frozen like people in the aftermath of an explosion, each silently calculating their survival chances in lives that must grind on. The air vibrated. At last Mrs. Hicks turned her red eyes on Dakotah.

"You're his wife," she said.

There was no answer to that and Dakotah felt her own hooves slip and the beginning descent into the dark, watery mud.

ABOUT THE AUTHOR

Annie Proulx is the author of *The Shipping News* and three other novels, *That Old Ace in the Hole, Postcards,* and *Accordion Crimes,* and the story collections *Heart Songs, Close Range,* and *Bad Dirt.* She has won the Pulitzer Prize, a National Book Award, the *Irish Times* International Fiction Prize, and the PEN/Faulkner Award, and was recently inducted into the American Academy of Arts and Letters. She lives in Wyoming.